ight, Miss Nelson?"

Asher moved to her side, bending to peer into her face. "You look flushed. You aren't taking ill, are you?"

His proximity wasn't helping a bit. "No, it's just the heat of the store. I'll be fine once I step outside."

Gracious, what could she say without letting Asher know how much he affected her? She marched out the door.

"Miss Nelson!"

Charlotte froze and closed her eyes. She'd walked out and forgotten her purchases. Oh, that man did fluster her. She needed to devise a way to keep clear of him, or she'd lose her mind. She turned and reentered the store, grabbing her package from the sheriff's hands. "Thank you."

"Miss Nelson," Mrs. Mabry called after her when Charlotte again headed for the door. "Do you want me to put those on your credit?"

"Yes, please." Never in her life had Charlotte charged anything, but she could not go back in the store. Not with Asher's gaze resting on her like hot coals, or the way he smelled. Goodness, but the man smelled like smoke, fresh air, pine and something all him that, mixed together, wreaked havoc on her senses.

Books by Cynthia Hickey

Love Inspired Heartsong Presents

Cooking Up Love
Taming the Sheriff

CYNTHIA HICKEY

Multipublished author Cynthia Hickey is represented by the MacGregor Literary Agency. Her first novel, a cozy mystery, was released in 2007, and she hasn't stopped publishing since. Writing is like breathing for her. Cynthia lives in Arizona with her husband, one of their seven children, two dogs, two cats and a fish named Floyd. She has five grandchildren, who keep her busy and tell everyone they know that "Nana is a writer." Visit her website at www.cynthiahickey.com.

CYNTHIA HICKEY

Taming the Sheriff

HEARTSONG
PRESENTS

Recycling programs
for this product may
not exist in your area.

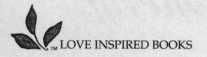 LOVE INSPIRED BOOKS

ISBN-13: 978-0-373-48680-9

TAMING THE SHERIFF

Copyright © 2013 by Cynthia M. Hickey

www.Harlequin.com

Printed in U.S.A.

Trust in the Lord with all your heart, and do not trust in your own understanding. Agree with Him in all your ways, and He will make your paths straight.

—*Proverbs* 3:5–6

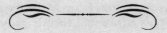

To God
for His neverending ideas

To my husband
for his unlimited support

To my agent, Chip MacGregor,
for his advice and encouragement

To my editor, Kathy Davis,
for taking another chance on me

And to my readers…
You are the ones who make this possible

Chapter 1

Ozark Mountains, 1881

No turning back now.

Charlotte Nelson glared at the drunken man—Hiram Something—beside her. Squaring her shoulders, she gripped the reins and eyed the white expanse between the trees. While snow blurred lines of the landscape, dotting Charlotte's eyelashes and numbing her fingers, Hiram snored from the wagon seat. Charlotte shivered so hard she thought her bones would come through her skin. She fought the impulse to plant an elbow squarely in his ribs.

Were they still on the road? How could she tell with all the snow? They had to be lost. Her heart seized.

What little light they'd had was gone. Clouds covered the sky, blocking out any stars flickering overhead. Spiders crept up her spine. She was lost in unfamiliar territory with an unconscious stranger. Not how she envisioned spending her first night in a new town.

"Yah!" She snapped the reins to encourage the mules to pick up the pace. She might have been a fly buzzing around them for all the good it did. "Brrr." She glared at her erstwhile driver. He sat with his head tossed back, mouth gaping. Would the fool freeze to death despite the alcohol in his system?

Charlotte groaned and freed one hand so she could dig behind the seat for a blanket. Her fingers grasped a rough wool one. Pulling it across Hiram, she wrinkled her nose at the strong horse odor. At least *she* was conscious…for now. The way her blood boiled, she should keep warm even under these circumstances.

"Come on, you miserable beasts." She slapped the reins again. The animals plodded forward with all the speed of molasses running uphill in the winter. Charlotte's breath escaped her in a wispy fog.

Please, Lord, let us be headed in the right direction. Maybe she should have asked for a map to Plumville when she got off the train. She glared at Hiram again. Since she was supposed to have a driver, she shouldn't have needed a map.

Charlotte frowned and wished for thicker gloves. She removed one hand from the reins and slid it under her thigh, hoping her body heat would thaw her fingers. What if she were stuck out here all night, driving in circles? She'd be part of the landscape by morning.

No. She wouldn't panic. She'd have to tough it out. If her parents knew she drove through a blizzard with a drunkard, they'd say, "I told you so," and cart her home to Georgia as fast as a train could carry her.

They didn't understand their oldest daughter's drive to be a teacher. In their minds, she should be back home learning to run a house and keep a husband happy. Even with the end of the War Between the States, and the loss of their fine plantation, Charlotte's mother still insisted on Southern gentility. After all, her father was now a businessman, the owner of a mercantile. Charlotte couldn't have been more different from her parents. She counted it a blessing that a teaching job became available midterm, even if it *was* in a hollow in the Ozark Mountains. Waiting until next fall would have meant almost a year of her mother badgering her about her choice of a career over marriage.

A sliver of light glimmered through the trees. A house? Charlotte leaned forward and peered through the gloom. It was! *Thank You, God.*

She pulled as close to the house as possible and set the brake.

"Uncle Asher! Matthew took the last biscuit." Luke crossed his arms and frowned. "Widow Slater won't make more till next week."

"Ain't my fault I'm still hungry." Matthew tossed his brother a bite of bread as if he was throwing food to a dog.

Mark, the quiet middle child, caught the piece in midair and popped it in his mouth while Luke howled.

Asher Thomas gulped his coffee and fought the urge to smack all three of his nephews upside the head until they quit arguing. Sometimes, it didn't take a lot of guesswork to see why his brother took off after his wife died.

His nephews grinned. Despite his aggravation, Asher grinned back. How could he hold a grudge against three freckled boys who looked so much like him and his brother at their age? Nah, he loved the scoundrels, re-

gardless of their shenanigans, and fighting over a biscuit didn't really warrant a spanking.

Someone pounded on the front door. Asher glanced
around the now silent table.

Matthew shrugged. "Guess you oughta answer it,
Uncle. Might be important."

"Of course I'll answer it." Asher pushed to his feet.
"I'm the sheriff, after all."

Asher parted the faded gingham at the window
and peered out into the storm. He saw only a body
slumped in a wagon seat under the overhanging eaves.
Was someone hurt? Asher grabbed his rifle from the
mantel, then swung the door open.

"Thank the Lord!" A woman who barely reached
Asher's shoulder brushed past him. "It's colder than a
brass doorknob in January out there. Could you help
the fool on the seat get out of the wagon? He's inebri-
ated." She removed a dark wool cloak, scattering snow
across the floor as she made a beeline for the fireplace.

Asher stared, openmouthed at raven curls falling
free from a bun. Eyes the color of a winter sky twinkled at him.

"Are you deaf? I know a little sign language, but not
much. Maybe you read lips?" She enunciated slowly
then smiled to take some of the sting out of her words.

He could read her lips just fine. As they warmed,
her lips pinked to the color of cherries and tilted at the
corners. The huskiness of her voice sent tingles down
his spine.

Asher shook his head in an attempt to distract his
thoughts. "I'm not deaf. Name's Asher Thomas. I'm
the sheriff around here. These are my nephews, Matthew, Mark and Luke. My brother didn't have a chance

to get a John." Why in the world was he blathering like an idiot? "I'll, uh, get your friend."

"Thank you." She moved closer to the fireplace and held out her hands. Steam rose from the damp hem of her skirt.

Asher dragged his attention away from her shapely form and stepped outside. Hunching his shoulders against the unfriendly weather, he made his way to the wagon. The man grunted as Asher pulled him from the seat. Whiskey fumes washed over Asher's face, and he wrinkled his nose. He shoved his shoulder under the man's arm, then dragged him into the house.

Their pretty guest had poured herself a cup of coffee. "I hope you don't mind. The boys offered, and, well, I'm feeling a bit like an icicle."

Asher shook his head and propped the drunken man in the corner near the fireplace. "Help yourself. There's stew in the pot if you'd like."

"Oh, I would. Bless you!" She scurried to the cast-iron kettle and sniffed. "Delightful!"

Did she say everything as an exclamation? Asher snapped his fingers and motioned for one of the boys to fetch a tin plate. "Ma'am, you're more than welcome to anything I might have, but I'd like to know your name. And the name of that fella in the corner. Also, could you tell me why the two of you are out in this storm?"

"I'm Charlotte Nelson, Plumville's new school-teacher. That's the man hired to drive me to town. His name is Hiram."

Asher's blood boiled. The school board had hired a drunk to deliver the new teacher? Of all the stupid things he'd ever seen. "My apologies, miss. I'm sure nobody knew the man would arrive in this condition."

If the night wasn't blowing so cold, Asher would haul him to jail that instant.

"Well, I'm here now—wherever here is." Her grin almost jerked the rug out from under him. A person would think he'd never seen a pretty girl before. He shuffled his feet.

"You're in Plumville, or at least the outskirts." Asher cast a wary glance at his silent nephews. As soon as Charlotte had told them who she was, they'd stopped chattering. Asher could almost see the wheels turning in their heads. He needed to get the woman to her home. Fast.

"Your place is half a mile from here. Leave Hiram where he is, and once you've finished eating, I can take you the rest of the way."

Her face brightened. "That would be wonderful." She turned to the boys. "Will the three of you be my students?"

Matthew grinned and nodded toward his brothers. "Yes, ma'am. And we're right excited."

Asher grabbed Charlotte's cloak. "You can finish eating in the wagon. We'd best be going." He threw the cloak around her shoulders and steered her toward the door, glaring at the boys over his shoulder. "Storm doesn't appear to be letting up. Can't waste any more time."

"All right." She waved at the boys. "See you on Monday."

"Bye," they said in unison.

"You boys be good." Asher closed the door firmly behind him. If Charlotte knew his nephews were the reason Plumville needed a new teacher in the first place, she might run screaming into the night.

The good-looking sheriff, with hair like wheat and eyes the color of summer grass, didn't talk much. When he did, he stammered like a boy just out of short pants. Endearing, really.

Charlotte shrugged and hugged her waist. She couldn't wait to get to her new home and start a fire in the stove. She already missed the milder weather of home. "Does the temperature usually drop this low in October?"

"Nope. Freak storm. It'll be gone in a few days." He rubbed the stubble on his chin.

Charlotte studied Asher's chiseled profile. My, but he was handsome. A lot different from the men back home. More rugged. Earthy. "Is there a lot of crime in Plumville? Why doesn't the town just use the sheriff from Fayetteville? You don't have a large population, correct?"

"Got an ongoing feud that causes a problem once in a while." He swished the reins. "But nothing the teacher needs to worry about. You're here to teach all the children in the hollow. Folks understand that."

A feud? Goodness. Visions of gun-toting outlaws drawing lines in the dirt filled Charlotte's mind. She buried her chin in her cloak. Wouldn't it be wonderful if God used her to repair the rift between these warring people? Her parents always said she possessed the ability to bring people together. She shivered with anticipation more than the temperature. Her new future looked brighter and brighter. Finally, she could make a difference in people's lives.

Of course, Mother always said Charlotte jumped into things without looking, too.

"Here we are." The wagon halted.

Charlotte uncovered her face and stared. She hadn't expected much, accepting a job in the Ozarks, but this building was barely larger than her bedroom back home.

"Over there is the schoolhouse. Might need some work." Asher climbed from his seat and hoisted one of Charlotte's trunks on his broad shoulders. "Show me where you want these, and I'll head on home."

"Oh." Charlotte frowned when it became obvious the sheriff wasn't going to offer her a hand down. Chivalry was dead in Plumville. She climbed awkwardly to the ground and marched toward her new home. She'd check out the school in the morning. Now that the first leg of her adventure had come to a close, weariness weighted her limbs.

A lantern sat on the step. Asher lit the wick and handed the foul-smelling thing to her. She pushed at the door, and it creaked open. Snow danced across the floor, mingling with at least an inch of dust. A stone fireplace took up most of one wall, complete with a swivel hook for hanging a cooking pot. No stove, but Charlotte could get along fine with only a fire.

Along the opposite wall ran a wooden counter with shelves full of canned goods. A bed, with an obvious lumpy mattress, was shoved in a corner. A rocking chair invited a body to relax by the fire's glow, and a small, round table surrounded by four cane-bottom chairs finished the furnishings. Cozy. Or it would be once she unpacked her things.

Charlotte rushed to the hearth. "Once I get a fire going, the place will be perfect. Just set the trunks anywhere, please, and thank you."

Asher brushed past her, balancing the trunk on his shoulder. "Let me take care of the fire, then I'll fetch your other trunk. There should be plenty of wood in the box there. The ladies in town made sure you had food and clean linens. Looks like they didn't have time to sweep."

Charlotte pulled her gaze away. They didn't make men like him back home. If her sister could see him she'd have to pick her jaw up off the floor after one glance. "That's all right. I can manage, and I appreciate all they did have time to do." With hands on her hips, she glanced around. "How far is the mercantile, just in case I forgot something I need? The school board sent me my first month's pay, and I'm itching to get started."

After shoving the trunk against a wall, Asher knelt and blew on a tiny spark he'd coaxed to life among the tinder. Thank goodness someone had been by to keep the wood smoldering. "Mabry's mercantile is about a twenty-minute walk. Take the path down the hill, go west up the mountain, turn right at the fork in the road. Can't miss it. Tomorrow, someone will be bringing you a mule that will help you get around." He stood, tipped his hat and scurried out the door as if Charlotte might take a broom to him. Within minutes, he'd returned with her other chest, deposited it beside her, said a quick goodbye and disappeared like the smoke up the chimney.

She shrugged, then spun in a circle, arms open wide. Hers! All hers, and she'd gotten the job herself, not because of Daddy's influence in the community. She dragged a chest closer to the fire and lifted the lid.

Dresses and books filled the inside. Charlotte glanced at the hooks over the bed. She might need a couple more to hang up all her clothes. Her weariness fled with the anticipation of settling into her own place. She grabbed a broom and swept, then arranged the contents of her trunks as best she could.

She put two more sticks of firewood on the blaze. The tiny cabin was warm now. She peered out the single window beside the door. Snowflakes drifted lazily to the ground. She would have loved to inspect the school, but only an empty-headed youngster would dash outside in this weather to explore an unfamiliar place in the dark. Instead, she grabbed one of her precious notebooks from the table. She could plan her first lesson at least.

After filling a battered tin pot with water and hanging it over the fire, Charlotte curled up with a quilt from home and chewed her fingernail. First thing would be to establish some sort of attendance record, then determine the students' grade levels. The school board's letter told her she could expect anywhere from ten to twenty students each day, depending on the time of year.

Well, Charlotte would do better than that. She'd insist on perfect attendance. The town would marvel at her ability to get the children to attend. She grinned. They'd wonder what they'd ever done without her.

She undressed quickly and dove under the blankets piled on the cornhusk mattress. Feeling like a butterfly encased in a cocoon, she snuggled down, closed her eyes and thanked God for the wonderful opportunity He'd given her.

Asher piled dishes from dinner in the wash sink and glanced at the loft where his nephews whispered. If Asher's guess was correct, they were hatching plans to scare the new schoolmarm back to where she'd come from. Their smiles scared him clear to his bones. The memories smarted: the last teacher had left the hills six weeks ago missing a tooth and sporting a bald patch on the back of his head.

The thought of Charlotte losing any of those curls that shone like a raven's feathers caused his heart to lurch. Of course, her teeth were nice, too. He groaned.

The last thing he needed, or had time for, was a pretty girl. Those hooligans above his head took all his spare time and then some. And the stupid feud took the time his nephews didn't.

He tossed a damp rag on the table and stomped to his favorite chair—a large, wood-framed one with a leather seat. He'd built it himself and didn't let anyone else take up residence in its ample arms. It was the only thing in the house off-limits to the boys. With a sigh of relief, he settled down and toed off his boots. He leaned his head back and closed his eyes, letting the fire's warmth seep into his bones.

Images of a pretty, dark-haired schoolmarm flickered on the backs of his eyelids. This wouldn't do. Sleep would be a long time coming, and he had more work to do the next day than he could possibly fit into daylight hours. He pushed to his feet then made his way to the cot he called a bed. Someday, he needed to get a bed made where his feet didn't hang off the edge. Maybe the same time he found a woman who didn't mind being married to a sheriff with three rowdy boys.

Hiram snored from the floor in front of the fire. Asher wrapped a pillow around his head and prayed for sleep.

Chapter 2

The next morning, Charlotte crawled out of bed to sunshine streaming through the window. Orange-red embers still glowed in the fireplace. Grabbing a shawl from the foot of her bed, she stuffed her feet into rabbit-fur-lined slippers and shuffled across the chilly floor to peer outside. Diamonds rode the sun's rays across an unbroken expanse of white, inviting her to romp.

"Oooh!" Charlotte slipped her feet in her boots, grabbed her thick coat, then dashed outside. The storm of the night before had left several inches of powdery softness blanketing the ground. She kicked it into a cloud as she raced across it. She wished it were deeper so she could throw herself down and make a snow angel.

She caught sight of the schoolhouse through the trees. It rose from the white blanket like a wizened old woman with graying doors and sagging shutters.

With a glance around to make sure no one was close

enough to spot her in her nightgown, Charlotte darted to the one-room building. She pushed open the door and stepped inside. Sunbeams splashed through the windows, dust motes shimmering.

Pine planks served as desks, long enough for three students to sit on each matching bench. A battered oak desk took up residence at the front of the room next to a wood-burning stove by the blackboard. Behind the desk, wood planks that dearly needed replacing let in pinpricks of light to dapple the floor.

Charlotte grinned at the sight of windows on the side walls, too small for anything other than a small child to squeeze through, but allowing enough light to see by. A dented brass bell sat proudly on the teacher's desk.

Charlotte clapped her hands. God had blessed her beyond measure. She couldn't wait to start school.

Now, how could she improve the situation? She twirled a finger in her hair. Hooks on the wall to hang coats and lunch pails. One of the desks leaned to one side. She'd ask the sheriff to get someone to fix that.

A small stack of firewood lay next to the stove. Curious to see whether anyone bothered to lay a fire, Charlotte opened the stove door. Two beady eyes peered up at her. She screamed and dashed outside, stopping only when she rammed into a red-and-black-checkered flannel wall.

Asher put out his hands to steady her and raised his eyebrows as he looked over her shoulder.

"There is a—" Charlotte gulped air and pointed to the school "—creature in the stove. Almost bit me. Scared me out of my mind."

Asher's gaze ran over her, and his face paled. He set her aside and marched into the school. Seconds later, a raccoon scurried out. Asher followed, stood to the side of the building and stared at the roof.

Charlotte joined him. "What are you looking at?"

"Flue was left open."

"Well, do you think the animal has rabies?"

"Rabies?" He shook his head. "He doesn't appear to be sick, and he wasn't going to hurt you."

Goodness! Charlotte clutched her coat with one hand. Her face burned hotter than the summer sun. What must he think of her? "Wait here." She sprinted for the house.

She prayed he wasn't a gossiping man. Although her nightgown was thick to guard against winter's chill and most of it was covered by her thick wool coat, the last thing she needed was for the parents of her students to think her a wanton woman.

After throwing on a dress and tying back her mane, she swung the pot of water over the coals, tossed on another log, took a deep breath and then marched back out to where Asher stood like a frozen sculpture.

"I've water boiling. Would you like some coffee?" Charlotte forced her features into a calm mask. No sense letting him know how embarrassed she remained.

He nodded. "I reckon that would be all right." He started to follow her inside, then stopped at the door. "I'll have mine out here."

"But it's freezing. Oh." She'd done it again. The poor man must think the school board scrounged the dregs of society looking for their next teacher. Of course he couldn't come in without proper chaperonage. Especially so early in the morning. "Why don't you get the boys, and I'll fix all of us some breakfast?"

Asher nodded and rushed away like a mad animal was on his heels.

Charlotte laughed. She did seem to have that effect

on men. They didn't tend to stick around long after she took to speaking her mind. She'd never figure them out. Not in a month of Sundays.

When he realized Charlotte wore her nightgown beneath her coat, Asher thought his heart would stop. Sure, it hid every inch of her and was covered with a thick winter coat, but it had lace and ruffles and her hair fell to her waist like a black river…he couldn't get out of there fast enough. What kind of woman did they hire? Would the boys be safe around her? She seemed all right, just strange, and kind of…uninhibited.

He launched himself onto the back of his horse, Samson, and galloped home as fast as the mountain trail would allow. The boys would be thrilled with a meal cooked by someone other than him, and he prayed they'd be on their best behavior.

Matthew, Mark and Luke whooped and hollered when Asher told them they were going to Miss Charlotte's for breakfast. "Scrub your faces till they shine and slick back your hair."

Mark glared. "Come on, Uncle Asher, the teacher won't care that we don't look like city fellers."

"No, but she'll mind whether you're clean or dirty. Now git. We don't want to keep her waiting."

Taking his own advice, he studied his reflection in the bucket of water outside the door, then licked his hand and flattened a strand of hair that insisted on sticking straight up. "Come on, boys. It takes fifteen minutes to get there."

"Hold your horses." Matthew sprinted past him. "You ain't got the wagon hitched yet."

Asher slapped his forehead. Instead of standing

around hollering orders, he should have hooked up the mule. "Come help."

Almost an hour passed by the time they arrived back at Charlotte's. The delightful smell of biscuits drifted on the breeze, welcoming them. When was the last time they ate fresh biscuits and not the leftovers the widow sent over? The four Thomas men hardly waited for the wagon to stop before piling out and banging on Charlotte's door.

She greeted them looking prettier than a picture in a ruffled yellow apron. Asher's mouth dried up.

"Perfect timing. Hope y'all like biscuits. I couldn't find any meat, but the white gravy's thick." Charlotte smiled and waved them inside. The boys bounced up and down as they scrambled for position around the table.

Asher would make sure she had meat by tomorrow and a couple extra chairs. "We'd be happy to eat just about anything." He clenched his jaw at the sight of three ruffians fighting over a basket in the center of the table. Charlotte firmly moved the biscuits away. "Gentlemen, we do not act this way. We sit at the table and say prayers first. Then we pass the basket like civilized folk." She narrowed her eyes. "Understood?"

They nodded. "Yes, ma'am."

Asher lowered into his seat. How'd she do that? Maybe he should watch how she interacted with them and see if he could learn something. Ever since his brother, Peter, had dropped the boys on Asher's doorstep, Asher hadn't known which end was up.

As soon as Charlotte replaced the basket and turned her back to fetch the gravy, his nephews started punching and shoving each other. Without turning around, she said, "Stop this instant or no breakfast."

Asher's mouth fell open when the boys straightened and sat still. Could it be that easy? No, there had to be a trick. Something he wasn't seeing. He watched as she flitted from the fireplace to the table and back to the fireplace. What would it be like to have a woman around the house all the time? Wonderful, he thought. But not just any woman. It had to be someone who could handle the boys and cook. Cooking was top priority.

Finally, Charlotte joined them at the table and held out her hands. When the boys hesitated to grasp hers, she wiggled her fingers.

"Let us pray." She waited until every head bowed before beginning. "Heavenly Father, thank You for this food, this roof over our heads and this fine company. Amen."

Asher could hardly concentrate on the blessing. His large hand dwarfed her soft, small one and left him feeling like a clumsy oaf.

"Now—" Charlotte handed him the biscuits "—I have to confess I have an ulterior motive for inviting you for breakfast. Two, actually." She grinned, stopping Asher's heart. "First, thank you for not laughing at my foolish behavior over the coon." The boys snickered. "Secondly, there are a few improvements I would like to make to the school before we start on Monday. That gives the weekend for the repairs. Do the board members have a list of people I can call on?"

"I can take care of things for you." Asher wanted to bite off his tongue. When was he supposed to find the time?

"Wonderful. I wrote them down." She dug a slip of paper out of her pocket.

No fewer than ten *improvements*. He really needed

to learn not to let a pretty face coerce him into doing things he didn't have time for.

When he looked up, Luke had a spoonful of gravy ready to flick at Miss Charlotte.

Charlotte merely held out her hand to Luke. "I'll take that, thank you." Luke scowled and gave up the spoon.

The little monsters didn't have her fooled for a minute. She'd heard their whispers before breakfast about locking the raccoon inside the schoolhouse as a welcome to the new teacher. How long had the poor creature been trapped?

Regardless, she'd mind her manners. She needed to gain control at the beginning, and keep it, or she'd fail at her dream of teaching before the first day. She refused to return to Georgia with her tail between her legs and let her family know they were right about her inability to be successful without Daddy's influence. It wasn't as if men had lined up at the door to marry her. Not with her strong will and her love of sharing knowledge. Teaching was the perfect career for her.

With breakfast over, Charlotte pushed back from the table and planted her fists on her hips. She eyed each of the boys with as stern a look as she could muster. "Since you three seem to have so much excess energy, I'll let you clear off the table. Just stack the dishes on the counter. If I see too much tomfoolery, I'll find another chore for you to do." She thanked the Lord she'd thought ahead far enough to purchase a setting for eight of the white speckled dishes. She'd like to occasionally invite her neighbors and students for supper.

Their eyes widened right along with Asher's. Charlotte bit her lip to prevent grinning and removed her apron. She grabbed her wool coat from a nearby hook and slipped her arms into the sleeves. "While y'all do that, I think I'll take a broom to the schoolroom."

Asher followed her out the door. "Should you leave them unsupervised?"

"If you don't give them the opportunity to prove themselves, they never will, Mr. Thomas."

He narrowed his eyes. "You don't know what they're capable of, *Miss* Nelson." His lip curled. "Or may I call you Charlie. Short for Charlotte."

Her eyes flashed. "No, you may not, and I think I do know what they're capable of. They're only little boys. What could they possibly do?" She knew how children behaved. Her extended family contained many cousins of all ages and both genders.

"I'll see about getting some help for your repairs." Asher tilted his hat and headed back inside the cabin.

Charlotte cringed at the sound of tin dishes clattering to the floor. "Well, at least I kept my china tea set packed in the trunk."

She rushed inside the school and set to work, sweeping hard enough to send a cloud of dust into the air. Coughing, she wiped her streaming eyes and slowed her pace, even though her insides still burned at Asher's insinuation that she didn't understand boys. She glared out the window as he and the three scoundrels climbed into the wagon and rumbled down the road.

By the time she'd finished preliminary cleaning, the sun hung high above the hollow, raising the day's temperature and melting the snow. Charlotte's stomach growled. She needed to go to the store and purchase supplies, and since no one bothered to drop off the mule Asher had told her about, she'd have to walk.

After exchanging her coat for a shawl, she strolled

in the direction Asher pointed out to her the day before. She hoped it would lead to the mercantile.

Wagon wheels left ruts in the road and tracks clear of grass and weeds. Yesterday's snow had melted, leaving patches of brown through the remaining white. Charlotte's boots squished, and she did her best to walk on the side of the trail. A cardinal flitted from branch to branch in a pine tree, its scarlet feathers a bright contrast to its surroundings.

Charlotte took a deep breath, the crisp air filling her lungs and her spirit. "Thank You, Lord, for setting me in such a lovely place." She shivered at the thought that she could have landed somewhere barren, like the desert. But she would have chosen even a place like that if it helped her reach her goal of independence.

By the time she reached the mercantile, her nose and cheeks felt chafed by the wind, but her insides were warm with the pleasure of having achieved what she set out to do. Teach young minds.

Two women in simple homespun skirts and knitted shawls exited the store.

"Good morning," Charlotte sang. "I'm the new schoolteacher." She held out her hand.

They glanced at her offering, then continued down the road with quick steps, reminding Charlotte of a couple of chickens heading to the hen house.

Charlotte pursed her lips. This community surely contained a lot of shy people. She pushed open the door and stepped into the warm mercantile.

The sour smell of salt brine and pickles filled the air, along with the scents of saddle soap, tobacco and beeswax candles. Shelves lined the walls with bolts of fabric, boxes of nails and other household necessities.

She loved browsing general stores. One never knew what treasure was hidden among the stores of goods.

She nodded at two gentlemen with whiskers flowing halfway down their chests. They stared for a second before returning to their game of checkers. Charlotte raised her eyebrows. Maybe it wasn't shyness that kept the people from responding. Maybe it was her. Her spirits fell as tears stung her eyes. Would she be alone, only receiving human companionship on school days? Surely not. She just needed to try harder.

She approached the two gentlemen hunched over the hand-carved game board, which sat on top of a pickle barrel. "Good morning. I'm Miss Nelson, the new teacher."

One man paused in moving his game piece. "Whose side you on, Jones or Sweeney?"

"Excuse me? I'm not on anyone's side." She glanced at the counter where a heavyset woman watched with crossed arms.

"The old coot is referring to the decade-old feud between the two families." She stepped around the corner. "I'm Mabel Mabry. This is my husband's store. What can I get you?"

"A feud?" Charlotte had thought for sure that Asher had been joking.

"Yep, and that right there is Hank Jones. Duke Sweeney won't step foot in here while he's in and vice versa. Puts a damper on business some days."

"Darn tootin'." Hank jumped his opponent's playing piece.

Goodness. Charlotte raised a hand to her throat. "Why are they so unfriendly toward me?"

Mabel shrugged. "Hill folk don't always take kindly to newcomers."

"Oh. Do they send their children to school?"

"Most of the time."

Charlotte leaned closer and whispered, "Whose side are you on?"

Mabel chuckled. "Whichever side is spending money in my store."

So it *was* possible to remain neutral. Charlotte sighed. What would a classroom full of Joneses and Sweeneys be like?

"I need some eggs, milk, flour, sugar, lamp oil and—" she tapped her finger on the counter as she searched her memory "—chalk and pencils. Please."

"Not sure we got the chalk and pencils." Mabel went behind the counter and bent to look on a low shelf. "Yep. One box of each left. You might want to order some from back east. It'll take about a month to get here, though."

Maybe Charlotte could write her parents and ask them to send supplies. Their church enjoyed helping out charities. Why not one of their own? She'd brought a supply of hand-crafted stationery from home. What better use could she find for it? After all, a donation from them wouldn't really count as not succeeding on her own, would it? The supplies would be for the students, not her.

She paid for her purchases and moved toward the door.

"Best decide whether you're a Jones or a Sweeney, girlie. Will make your life easier," Hank called.

Charlotte paused, then straightened her shoulders and rushed outside.

Asher rode Samson and led a blue-roan mule toward Charlotte's. He should have brought it yesterday, but until winter really set in, walking should suit the schoolteacher fine. Most folks walked in the hollow and she'd need to fit in.

He found her sitting on the top step of the schoolhouse, her eyes red-rimmed and her mouth turned down. "Why the long face?"

She bit her bottom lip. "Why is there a feud between the Jones and Sweeney families? I was at the mercantile today and people were very unfriendly to me. Don't they want a teacher?" Her eyes shimmered, causing his throat to swell.

Asher gulped. She wasn't going to cry, was she? Wanting to turn Samson around, he climbed down instead. "I brought your mule. His name's Blue."

She sniffed. "Thanks."

"The feud started with Hank's and Duke's fathers." Asher sat beside her. "Age-old story of two men fighting over a pretty gal. Turns out she ran off with a third fella, but the two old coots have hated each other ever since. Used to be best friends once."

"That's silly." Charlotte wiped her face on her sleeve.

"Yep." He stared across the yard, anywhere but at the rosy cheeks and crazy curls of Charlotte Nelson. Looking at her made it easy to see why men would come to blows over a woman. But not him. There wasn't room in his life for anyone. At least not until Asher located his no-good, gambling brother and dragged his sorry carcass home to face his three high-spirited responsibilities.

Besides, what woman in her right mind would court the sheriff of a small hill town that was at war with itself? "Folks'll warm up to you. Just give them time."

"But will they send their children to school?" Charlotte propped her chin in her hands. "That's the most important thing."

"Sure they will. Some of them might be backward in their way of thinking, but most know the benefits of an education." Asher's own parents had made sure he attended school every day possible. He could never thank them enough for the sacrifices they made.

"What about your nephews? They hate me."

Asher snorted. "No, they don't. They're just wild. I don't think they've had much consistency even before their dad took off. They've had a rough time of it, but I'm doing the best I can." He watched her face for signs of condemnation. He felt like he could do more for the boys, but didn't have a clue what. Maybe stay home more, but he had a job to do. Peace to keep. At twelve, Matthew should be plenty old enough to supervise the younger boys.

Charlotte jumped to her feet and clapped her hands. "I know exactly what I'll do." She grinned. "I'll direct a Christmas play with all my students in it. Not only will it be fun, but it will draw the town closer together."

The cold must have addled her brain. A play that involved the Joneses *and* the Sweeneys under the same roof? "It won't work."

Her smile faded. "Why not?"

"Folks'll shoot each other. They'll fight over the parts they think their child should have."

"There won't be any bad parts. Not for older students, anyway." Charlotte crossed her arms. "They'll see reason once they see how excited the children are. I'd like your nephews to play the three Magi. It will teach them responsibility."

Asher stood and headed for his horse. "Suit yourself,

but don't come crying to me when you find yourself beating your head against the wall."

"Don't worry, Mr. Thomas. I won't bother you for a thing."

He turned as she stomped her foot and whirled to dash into the cabin. He did admire her spirit. With a face-splitting grin of his own, he swung into the saddle and headed Samson in the direction of the mercantile. Yep, it really was too bad he wasn't looking for a woman. Charlotte Nelson would fit him perfectly.

Samson's long legs ate up the distance, and Asher welcomed the warmth of Mabry's store. He tipped his hat at Hank Jones and his partner as he entered. "Gentlemen."

"Sheriff." Hank nodded. "Teacher was here a while ago."

Asher set his lips in a firm line. "Heard y'all weren't too friendly."

"Way I see it, she ain't bigger than a minute. Most of the students will walk all over her. Won't be here long enough for us to care." Hank faced Asher. "And she didn't choose a side. Everyone chooses."

"I haven't." Asher pushed his hat back.

"That's 'cause you're the lawman. You can't, but she can."

Asher shook his head. "A teacher treats all their students the same. Miss Nelson will, too. You'd best get over your grievances. She plans on putting on a Christmas pageant."

"A what?"

"A play."

"What for?"

Asher took a deep breath and squared his shoulders. "To draw the town closer together."

"When cows sprout wings!" Hank grabbed his gun. "Ain't no two-foot-high teacher gonna tell me and mine what to do. I'll take care of that right now. I aim to give that teacher a talking to."

Chapter 3

Monday morning, Charlotte stood on the top step in front of the school and rang the cowbell to signal the start of a new day. Fifteen students, carrying tin lunch pails, shoved past her and jostled for seats nearest the stove. Instead of sitting boys to one side, girls on the other, as was customary, they clearly chose by family. Only two strode to the front and divided on to each side.

Despite the cold creeping between cracks in the walls, the room's warmth invited Charlotte to discard her cloak. She glanced at the blackboard where she'd written her name in her best penmanship. She grinned. At last. What she'd waited years for. The first day as a teacher.

She made her way to the front and turned to face the class. Holding one finger over her mouth, with the other hand she pointed to the ceiling with two fingers. She waited several minutes without speaking until the students noticed her signal. When she had their attention, she spoke. "This is the sign I will show when I want your attention and for you to quiet." She smiled. "I am Miss Nelson. First thing on today's agenda will be to take roll and determine your grade placements."

Amidst grumbling, roll call ate away the first twenty minutes of the morning. Then, Charlotte divided the students with the youngest in front and the oldest in the back of the room. She noted with satisfaction the division of the Thomas brothers. Their separation should work to her advantage.

"I can't sit by no Sweeney!" A dark-haired boy of about eight glared at the blond boy next to him who promptly followed that a Jones smelled worse than a skunk.

"Students, really." While still maintaining some semblance of order, Charlotte moved the feuding students farther apart. She wouldn't give in to their silly actions, but didn't want to start the first day with a riot, either. She'd mend the breach between them all soon enough.

The feuding families sat in desks as far away from each other as possible, except for a pretty blonde girl and a boy with hair the color of mahogany. They sat on the end seat of their rows and only seemed to have eyes for each other.

With the older students practicing multiplication, Charlotte pulled up a rickety wooden chair and focused on the younger ones and their reading. By the day's end, she wanted to know where each student stood academically.

A pencil flew across the room and plunked against the chalkboard. Charlotte raised her eyes from the reader on the desk in front of her. She laid a hand on the shoulder of the little girl next to her to keep the child calm. Snickers came from the back of the room.

"Go back to your seat and practice writing the alphabet. You're doing wonderfully." Charlotte stood and erased the chalkboard. At times like these, she'd give almost anything to have eyes in the back of her head. She suspected the culprits were none other than Matthew Thomas and his friends.

She turned and pretended to fiddle with the buttons on her boot while peeking under her arm toward Matthew. The boy drew back his arm and let another pencil fly, barely missing Charlotte's head. She snapped to attention. "Matthew Thomas! Approach my desk immediately."

With a smirk toward his buddies, Matthew shuffled to her desk. Without glancing at her, he mumbled, "My name is Matt."

"Matthew—" Charlotte narrowed her eyes "—you will fill the wood box after school, clean the blackboard and sweep the stoop as punishment for your shenanigans. Is that clear?"

"Yes, ma'am." He turned and plodded his way to his seat where he plopped down with a sullen expression and crossed his arms.

Charlotte wanted to be compassionate to the motherless boy, especially with his father gone, but she could not tolerate disobedient behavior in her classroom. She sighed, glancing at the sweet face of Luke. No. She must be kind but firm. Overly soft, and she'd have trouble a plenty.

At noon, Charlotte closed the book on her desk. "Thirty minutes for lunch and recess." The students stampeded outside, leaving her with a moment's peace. Their shouts drifted through the open door. Grabbing her lunch pail, Charlotte moved outdoors, too. She gathered her cloak against the chill and lifted her face to the winter sun.

So far, thank the Lord, the four students in her class from the feuding families kept to themselves. But the constant love-struck glances between Frank Jones and Lucy Sweeney were more than enough to cause concern. Especially if the stubborn family matriarchs caught wind of the teenagers' obvious infatuation with each other. Charlotte smiled. A regular Romeo and Juliet story worthy of William Shakespeare—an author she hoped to introduce these students to someday. But having it come to life in her classroom was a different story.

Frank snared Lucy's hand and tugged her toward the grove of trees.

"I don't think so, Mr. Jones." So much for the two families staying away from each other. Charlotte waved them back toward the school yard. "Stay where I can see you and please refrain from holding hands while at school."

She lifted her skirts high enough to keep them out of the dirt and headed to the outhouse. With five minutes left of lunchtime, she'd better hurry. She eyed the building with distaste.

Grasping the rope handle, she tugged the door open and stepped inside. Minutes later, mission accomplished, Charlotte pushed against the door. It refused to budge. "Hello?" She banged on the rough wood. "A little help, please. The door seems to be stuck."

No childish laughter greeted her cries for help. Charlotte plastered her cheek against the wall and peered through a crack. The scoundrels. Matthew and his brothers stared at the outhouse, grins across their faces. The other students were nowhere to be seen.

"Don't think I won't tell your uncle about this!" Charlotte kicked the planks. "Joke's over, boys. Let me out."

"Nope," one of them yelled.

Charlotte heard the thundering sounds of feet dashing in the opposite direction. Her shoulders slumped. She set back to study the worn planks that made up the outhouse walls. It might take a while, but she figured she could break through.

Asher stared at the telegram in his hand. What was he going to do about his brother? The description of one of the bank robbers sure sounded like Peter. The second robbery this month. Asher folded his hands behind his head and leaned back in his chair.

Could be coincidence. There must be plenty of blond-haired men with a scar down one cheek. But his gut told him Pete was most likely the culprit.

The boys barged through the door, and Asher let his chair fall into place. They stopped laughing for a moment, guilty looks on their faces, then skedaddled toward the ladder leaning to the loft.

"Hold up, boys." Asher stood. "How was the first day of school? The new teacher do all right?"

"Fine, Uncle Asher," Matthew said with a wide-eyed look at his brothers.

"Well, what did y'all do today? Learn anything new?"

"Nope. Not a thing." Matthew grabbed a rung.

"Nope." The other two echoed his words.

"Ya'll are out early." Asher frowned. Something smelled mighty fishy. "What did y'all do?"

"What do you mean?" Mark stepped behind his older

brother. "We told you, we didn't do nothing. Maybe a little arithmetic and some reading."

Asher crossed his arms. "Besides schoolwork. Where's Miss Nelson?"

"In the outhouse." Luke clapped his hand over his mouth.

"Explain." He shot a warning look to hush the older boys. "I want Luke to tell me. The truth now, ya hear?"

"It's just a joke." Luke grinned. "A funny one, too. We propped a board in front of the outhouse and now she's stuck like a porcupine in honey."

Heat rose up Asher's neck. "How long ago?"

Luke's smile faded. "Lunchtime."

"Two hours ago? Why didn't one of the other students let her out?"

Luke swallowed hard. "'Cause Matthew said he'd pound anyone that told."

Asher grabbed his coat from a nail on the wall. "You three go to the loft and stay there. I'll deal with you when I get back."

Heaven help the woman. He hoped she at least got locked in with her coat on. What went through the minds of those three scoundrels? They'd poured ink in the last teacher's coffee, staining the man's teeth black for a week. But that hadn't been the end of it. The last straw came when they plugged the chimney flue and filled his house with smoke. The man had fallen against the front stoop and knocked out his front tooth.

Asher had made the boys scrub the barn until it shined like a new penny, but it hadn't seemed to have worked very well. Maybe he needed to take them behind the woodshed. Although the thought of striking one of the boys made him cringe.

He saddled Samson. The boys were upset about their

ma dying and their pa taking off. He couldn't fault them for that. But their behavior couldn't be tolerated, or they could end up like their ne'er-do-well father. He swung a leg up and over the saddle, then steered his horse toward school. Chances were, once they realized they still had folks around that loved them, they'd straighten up without being paddled.

He pulled up in time to see Miss Nelson's head, then shoulders, poke from a hole in the side of the outhouse. While he watched from across the yard, she continued to wiggle and squirm until she finally collapsed in a heap on the ground. Asher jumped down and rushed to her side.

Grasping her arm, he helped her to her feet. She jerked away and fixed eyes full of fire on him.

"Those boys of yours locked me in the outhouse." She slapped against her skirt to dislodge dirt and pieces of wood, then speared him again with eyes that blazed hot enough to char his skin. "You have got to do something.

"Earlier, Matthew threw pencils at me. I gave him a list of chores to do. I guarantee not a one of them is completed. Instead, he and the rest of the students went home, most likely bullied into doing so by your nephews, and left me in that foul-smelling place to rot." Her eyes chilled and shimmered. "Now the outhouse is unusable because I had to kick a hole in the wall."

"I'm sorry. Really. I'll fix the outhouse wall. But discipline at the school is the responsibility of the teacher. I'll talk to them, but I can't promise anything. They're only acting up because—"

"Responsibility of the teacher?" What might have been the start of tears vanished in a blink. High spots of color showed on her cheeks.

Asher stepped back. How could such a little thing appear so dangerous? He sure was glad he wasn't one of his nephews. "Yes, ma'am. That's what the school board pays you for. Not that I won't punish them. Yes, ma'am, I have every intention of doing so, but you're the one here with them all day.

"My job is to make sure they have food, clothes and a roof over their heads. I'll talk to them about their behavior, don't worry, and they'll fix that outhouse for sure."

She stiffened like someone stuck a pine trunk down her back. "Well. That clears things up. Good day, Sheriff." She marched past him and into the schoolhouse.

Asher rubbed his chin. What in tarnation had he said to put a burr under her saddle?

Responsibility of the teacher, indeed! Her cheeks burned from the tears she'd shed, combined with the cold weather. Charlotte warmed herself by the stove before banking the coals. Thank goodness the walls of the outhouse were made out of thin wood and loose at that. Still, her nails had broken to the quick, and her hands sported more splinters than she wanted to count.

She sagged against the wall. How foolish she was to expect the sheriff to side with her in seeing the boys were disciplined. Had he been a responsible guardian in the first place, they wouldn't behave the way they did.

It wasn't that Charlotte didn't have compassion. She did. Her heart ached that the poor boys had no parents. But at their age, they knew right from wrong. There must be consequences for their actions. Even the Lord disciplined those He loved. How could Charlotte do less?

She would insist that all three boys be taken to the woodshed. As for the rest of the school, well, she could mull over it that evening and let them know in the morning what their punishment would be. If the Thomas men wanted a battle of wits, she'd give them one.

And she'd make sure she won.

The next morning, Charlotte glanced up from checking arithmetic answers. Through the window, she could see the Thomas boys filling the seams in the schoolhouse walls with rich Arkansas clay. She appreciated the note they'd handed her from their uncle. Maybe the sheriff was on her side after all.

The rest of the students, for leaving her locked up and scattering like chickens chased by a fox, were copying Bible verses from the blackboard. She supposed she could've taken the boys behind the building for a whooping, but physical labor seemed a bigger punishment. Especially so when she insisted they would continue to work through lunch recess. She'd never cottoned to physical discipline no matter how often she might recommend—or consider—it.

She dismissed class and smiled as they grabbed coats and lunch pails before dashing outside. She followed and poked her head around the building. "Five minutes' break, boys, then back to work."

"That ain't fair." Matthew frowned and tossed a handful of mud to the ground. "We oughta get to play, too."

"About as fair as you locking me up in the bitter cold. Your efforts today will help all of us learn in warmer comfort." Charlotte wrapped her shawl around her shoulders. "How were things at home? Did you get in a lot of trouble?"

"Nope. Hardly any. Uncle Asher just told us not to do it again and to fix the outhouse good as new." Matthew flashed a grin then he and his brothers raced to the steps to wolf down cold sandwiches.

Really? Charlotte drew a sharp breath through her nose. She had no problem doling out consequences for bad behavior at school, but it would be nice to receive support from a student's parent or guardian. She intended to speak with the sheriff about her concerns as soon as possible. She sighed. What did she want the boys to receive? A severe spanking? She wasn't willing to paddle them herself, maybe their uncle felt the same. Besides, she had no real idea of the type of tongue lashing they may have gotten.

The Thomas boys were easily the brightest in their age groups, as evidenced by their studies. She narrowed her eyes and caught Matthew tossing a handful of clay at Mark. The burnished-orange color stuck to the back of his coat like a burr to a saddle blanket. Charlotte sighed and marched out to stop them from falling into a full-fledged mud fight.

"Gentlemen, I have a proposition for you." She crossed her arms.

"What kind?" Matthew asked. He motioned for his brothers to drop their handfuls of clay.

"Well, I'd like you to clean up, come inside and I'll inform you at the same time I let the rest of the class know. I believe you will be excited."

"We don't got to work no more?" Luke wiped his runny nose on the sleeve of his coat.

"No, sir, you do not have to work anymore. Not if y'all accept my offer."

"We'll wait to see what you got to say." Matthew steered his brothers to the pump.

"Fair enough." Charlotte nodded and rang the bell for the other students to come inside.

They thundered inside and took their seats. Charlotte gazed upon their serious faces. She couldn't wait to give them the news. "Class, we are going to put on a Christmas program for the community."

Cheers rose.

Charlotte raised her hand for silence. "I will need shepherds, a Mary and a Joseph, three wise men and a choir of angels. There will be a part for everyone." She smiled at the Thomas boys. "Matthew, Mark and Luke will play the three wise men."

The three jumped to their feet. "We ain't wearing no girly robes!" Matthew glowered. "Not me or my brothers."

Charlotte squared her shoulders. "Are you calling Jesus girly?"

"We ain't talking about Jesus." Matthew plopped into his seat.

"Actually, we are." Charlotte leaned against her desk. "Christmas is a celebration of Jesus's birth. I'm not asking you to wear anything they didn't wear back in Biblical days." She scanned her students. "As the oldest students here, I would like to ask Lucy and Frank to play Mary and Joseph."

The class gave a collective gasp.

Luke raised his hand. "Are you sure, Miss Nelson? 'Cause their families don't get along."

"I'm aware of that, Luke. But there's no reason those of us within these four walls can't. Maybe we can be an example to others." Charlotte hoped she knew what she was doing. What if her plan to draw the community together didn't work? What if everyone thought her idea ridiculous? No, surely they'd had programs where they worked together before. "I'd also like you three Thomas boys to write the script."

"No way." Matthew's face reddened. "This is just more punishment."

"No, it isn't. Go through the book of Luke and come up with a script and Christmas carols to fill at least half an hour. I have faith in you." Her heart turned a somersault at the surprised look on his face.

Charlotte turned to the blackboard. "Now, if all of you could copy down today's spelling words, we'll get back to our academics."

By the time class was dismissed and Charlotte finished closing up the school, clouds had gathered, casting the late afternoon into an early dusk. Charlotte stood on the top step. The Thomas boys clustered on the ground below her.

"Why haven't you left? Are you waiting for your uncle?" Charlotte scanned the road, noting the rest of the students were long gone.

"No, ma'am. He's most likely riding down crooks," Mark said. "That is his job."

"But it's getting dark. Y'all can't walk home alone with the possibility of a storm. I'll walk with you. If it storms, I'll wait it out."

"We appreciate that, Miss Nelson," Matthew said with a grin. "Luke gets scared when it's dark." He elbowed his brother when the younger boy opened his mouth to speak. "And we'd like to show you a shortcut to our place."

"That is a wonderful idea. Thank you." The rascal had something up his sleeve, but Charlotte wouldn't sleep if she didn't make sure they made it home safe.

The wind picked up, whistling through the trees. Charlotte shivered as a few leaves skittered across the ground. Very few patches of snow lay in the shadows where the afternoon sun couldn't reach. Fearful the sky would unleash another snowstorm, or worse, icy rain, Charlotte ushered the boys ahead of her.

They darted into the trees and out of sight.

"Wait for me." She lifted her skirts and rushed after them. Their laughter drifted across the air and bounced around the hollow.

"Matthew, Mark, Luke?" Charlotte stopped and turned in a circle. How could she have gotten so lost in mere minutes? Every direction looked the same— trees reaching toward a gray sky pregnant with clouds. A brown ground dusted with frozen patches that led nowhere.

The scoundrels. No problem. She'd go back the way she came. She studied the ground behind her. Without the layer of snow, her boots left no tracks for her to follow. Her fears were confirmed when she felt the first drop of ice against her cheek.

She was lost.

Chapter 4

Asher reined in Samson and stared in confusion at his dark cabin. It might be late afternoon, but the cloud cover thrust the mountain into twilight. Where were those boys? They should have been home hours ago with smoke rising from the chimney and a simple meal on the table. He'd asked them this one time to watch out for themselves while he made a sweep of the mountain, and look what happened. Asher slid from the saddle and stormed inside.

"Matthew, Mark, Luke?" No tempting scent of supper nor the welcoming warmth of a fire greeted him. "Boys?" Was it possible Miss Nelson kept them this late, working at the school? He'd give her a piece of his mind if she had.

He marched back outside and swung onto his horse. His blood boiled, pushing back the cold. Only a fool city slicker would keep children late after school with rain coming. As night fell, so did the temperature. A thin layer of ice lay over the ground already and crunched under Samson's hooves. As he rode, he rehearsed in his mind the heated words he'd give Miss Nelson about her irresponsibility.

Asher hunkered deeper into his sheepskin-lined coat against the icy rain. After riding the mountain to make sure there weren't any feuding folks getting out of hand, he felt frozen clear to his bone, and had looked forward to relaxing in front of the fire.

School let out more than two hours ago. Now the sun was setting, and the boys had to walk home in sleet. It was inconceivable that a teacher would allow such a thing.

He pulled Samson to a halt in front of the school and dismounted, draping the reins over a fence post. No smoke curled from the chimney here, either. He turned the knob. Locked. "Miss Nelson?" Turning, he surveyed the empty school yard.

Uneasiness swept over him. Where could the woman be? Was it possible his nephews were up to their tricks and the schoolmarm had met with harm? They did lock her in the outhouse a few days ago, and considering the level of pranks they had pulled on the previous teacher, anything was possible. If they had done something, he'd forgo his aversion to spanking and deliver them all a stinging paddle or two.

Asher slumped against the building. What was he going to do with those boys? He'd failed miserably so far, giving in to their every whim because he felt sorry for them. Well, no more. He'd serve up consequences. He sure would miss them when they were gone, trouble or not. The cabin had been mighty quiet before they were dropped off over a year ago.

But the boys had the same makings of being outlaws, just like Asher's brother. He couldn't allow it.

He marched to Samson and swung back up into the saddle. Most likely the schoolmarm was back home, safe and warm beside her fire. By the time he reached her small cabin, dread crept along his spine. He dismounted and knocked on the door. When he didn't receive an answer, he cupped his hands around his eyes and peered through the window. Dark. No fire burned, no lantern illuminated the small room. Miss Nelson most likely wandered the woods, in the cold, at night, and most likely at the hands of the young scalawags he'd had a hand in raising.

Rain dripped off the wide brim of his hat. Clouds obscured the moon, casting the land into a gray darkness. Where should Asher begin looking? He steered Samson toward the towering oaks and pines behind Miss Nelson's cabin and rode deep into the woods.

"Miss Nelson!" He slid from his horse and studied the ground around him. If he wanted to lead someone from the school to home, ditching them in the process, he'd take them through…there. Four sets of footprints formed in the hard ground. The teacher couldn't be far. The boys would've scattered at the first opportunity, and only three sets of prints left the area. Poor woman.

If she'd turned and gone in that direction, she'd have seen her cabin as soon as she stepped past that clump of pine. His heart almost froze knowing she was no longer with the boys. Would he have to hunt them down, too?

Asher cupped his hands around his mouth. "Miss Nelson!"

"I'm here." She crawled from the debris of a fallen tree, hair in disarray around her face, and limbs trembling. Blue lips stood out from her overly pale face. "Your nephews are going to be the death of me."

Charlotte shivered so hard she bit her tongue, filling her mouth with the taste of metal. Good thing those three boys weren't anywhere near. She'd stuff them in the log and leave them for a while and see how they liked it.

Asher whipped off his heavy coat and slung it around her shoulders. She closed her eyes at the welcome warmth and leaned into him, his chest solid and comforting against her. "I'd like to go home now."

"There's no fire at your place. None at mine, either, but if I take you to my place you can stay wrapped up while I get a log burning, and I've got to see whether my nephews have returned. I think it best if I keep an eye on you. You were out in the cold awhile."

She shook her head. "It's not seemly. What will folks think?"

"Nobody's going to be out in this." He helped her onto Samson then mounted behind her. "Besides, those three boys will be all the chaperonage a person needs."

"You should take your coat back." She attempted to shrug it off until his hand on her shoulder stopped her. "You'll freeze."

"I'll be fine. We'll both hunker down in front of the fire and be right as rain soon enough." He clicked to Samson, and they set off. Half-frozen, the only other thing she could feel was concern over the man shivering behind her. Despite the frost in the air, she could feel his body heat through the coat over her shoulders. Once they trotted out of the woods, they thundered down the road to the Thomases' cabin.

The cold still shook her bones when they reached

Asher's home, and Charlotte's head nodded with fatigue. Would she ever be warm again? She should have stayed in Georgia as her parents had advised, warm and snug in her featherbed.

Asher slid from the horse and gathered her into his arms. After kicking open the front door, he stepped over the threshold and deposited her in a rocking chair beside the blazing fireplace. Heat pricked her frozen fingers. Hadn't he told her his cabin would be cold?

Asher glared at the ceiling, then lifted his coat from Charlotte's shoulders and knelt in front of her, taking her hands in his large calloused ones. He shivered.

Charlotte straightened. "Please, don your coat, Mr. Thomas. Feeling is returning to my fingers and toes, and you're half-frozen." His caring for her comfort, and his grasp of her hands, caused her to tingle more than anything else. A fine film of dust drifted from the loft, and she lifted her gaze to see three sets of eyes peering down.

She pulled her hands free. "Come here, boys."

Reluctantly, three nightshirt-clad boys climbed down the ladder and stood, heads hanging, in front of her.

Charlotte wrapped her shawl closer around her and narrowed her eyes. "You may not care much about my welfare, but look at your uncle." They turned. "He's half-frozen. Working all day, then coming out in a sleet storm to find me. You'll all be lucky if he doesn't catch pneumonia after giving me his coat as a gentleman should. Now——" she set the rocker into motion "——how do the three of you think we should deal with this situation?"

"Miss Nelson, I'll take care of——" Asher moved into a large leather chair and pulled a fraying afghan around his shoulders.

"Please." Charlotte held up a hand to interrupt. "It's the least I can do after you came out into the rain to find me. Let me begin again." Besides, to her way of thinking, the man showed a definite lack in the art of discipline. He might be able to run down criminals, but keeping control of three young boys seemed to be more than he could handle. "I'm waiting for your answer, boys."

"String us up by our toes?" Matthew suggested, his eyes twinkling.

"Pull out our hair one by one," Mark said. The corner of his mouth quirked.

Luke chewed the cuticle on his left thumb and stared at the floor.

Charlotte's back stiffened, and she spoke through gritted teeth. Her course at the normal school did not teach her how to handle consistently unruly boys. "Obviously you boys do not take me seriously. I will dwell on the situation overnight and inform you of your punishment at school tomorrow. Mr. Thomas, if you're warm enough, I'd like to go home now." She would not stay within slapping distance of the three children. Parentless or not, they needed a firm hand, and it looked as though she would have to be the one to give it.

"No, I reckon I'm still cold." Asher unfolded his long frame from the chair. "You young'uns scoot to bed. Me and the teacher will discuss your behavior over hot cups of coffee." He ruffled Luke's hair. "I'm glad to see y'all home safe, but tomorrow will not be a pleasant day for the three of you. I want you to think on the possible consequences."

Really? He wanted to help? Hope leaped in Charlotte's chest. Finally, she'd have the uncle's support. If so, then freezing inside a bug-infested log might be worth it. Well, not that many bugs had come out in the winter, but still, the experience had been unpleasant, and she'd be lucky not to develop a nasty cold.

She watched as Asher prepared the coffee. The man seemed to know his way around a kitchen. Surprising how deft he was, considering his size. She flushed, remembering how easily he'd lifted her onto his horse, and how comfortable she'd felt with his arms wrapped around her. "Thank you for coming to my rescue today."

He turned from pouring their drinks and handed her a mug. "You're welcome." He stared at the mug. "It's because of my nephews that you were left outside to begin with. Why didn't you follow the tracks back out? The ground was wet enough."

"Tracks? But I looked behind me and didn't find a thing."

"The boys' tracks, Miss Nelson. They were plain to see going in the opposite direction from where you wandered."

How could she have been so stupid? Of course she should have checked the entire ground.

He waved a hand toward a cane-bottom chair. "Go ahead and have a seat at the table. I'm sure you're hankering to tell me how you want to dish out punishment."

"Don't you?" Charlotte slid onto the bench. "You must think what the boys did was wrong." Steam rose from her ironstone mug, teasing her nostrils with the rich aroma of dark coffee.

Shrugging, Asher sat across from her. "Sure, I do. I also believe the boys didn't know the severity of their actions. Their father didn't do much in the discipline department, and they've been running wild. Why'd you keep them after school in this kind of weather?"

"They served their punishment during lunch. There

was no *after school*." Charlotte set her drink on the table with enough force to cause some of the coffee to splash over the rim. "Because of the promised storm, and since you were nowhere to be found, I offered to walk them home. Being abandoned in the woods is the thanks I got.

"If you hadn't found me, I would have died by morning. Same as the little prank with the outhouse." She took a deep breath to settle her temper. It wouldn't do any good to get into a shouting match with the town's sheriff. "Whether they knew the severity of their actions or not, the boys must be disciplined severely. One way or another they need to learn right from wrong."

"They know." His gaze pierced her over the rim of his mug. "They're choosing wrong, and I intend to deal with it. I think you need to do the same at school. The boys need to learn to respect you as their teacher. If we form a united front—"

"I agree. They must be made to make the right choices." She would not raise her voice. Definitely not. Ladies did not shout, according to Mother, and Charlotte valued being a lady. But if the sheriff didn't see reason… "Mr. Thomas, I assigned your nephews to write the script for our school play, and—"

"You're still going ahead with that?" He frowned.

"I most certainly am. Why shouldn't I?"

He shrugged. "I think it's a bad idea to involve the Joneses and the Sweeneys together in a community project. You're setting yourself up for failure."

"That is my choice. After all, the students attend school together. Surely the parents can be in the same room for an hour." She stood, leaving her coffee untouched. "I'd like to go now. I will think of some way to discipline the boys and let you know."

"I don't think you're hearing me, Miss Nelson. I told you I planned on—" He coughed, the sound as harsh as a bullfrog's call.

"Oh, I hear you just fine, Mr. Thomas." One excuse after another is what she heard. "I thank you for the coffee. Now, before you take ill, I need to be getting home."

After a silent ride home, escorted by a sullen-faced Asher, Charlotte burst through her front door in a dither, and slammed it behind her before the sheriff could follow. Obviously, she'd stepped on his toes. Well, somebody needed to take a firm hand with the boys. Before the war, Charlotte's nanny ruled with an iron will. When the family had to let the woman go during Reconstruction because of a lack of funds, Charlotte's mother continued raising Charlotte and her sister with the same strict guidelines. And they'd turned out just fine, thank you very much.

She hung her coat on a hook by the fireplace and knelt in front of the cold embers. Maybe a job in a warmer climate, with friendlier people, in a culture she understood, should have been her primary objective. Because this…was not the idyllic first job she'd envisioned.

Charlotte struck a match and lit the small pile of tinder. Within minutes a flame leaped among the wood, lighting her spirits and sending out the first tendrils of warmth into the room. She moved to the counter and unwrapped a biscuit left over from breakfast. It would have to suffice until morning. Fatigue weighed too heavily for her to muster the strength to cook.

She knew she ought to be more understanding toward the Thomas men. After all, the boys had no parents to speak of, and the handsome, if not dour, sheriff had braved an ice storm to come to her rescue. But she was telling the truth—she really felt she could have perished in the elements.

Charlotte held her hands over the flames and recalled the feel of the sheriff's arms around her as they'd raced on his horse to his cabin. The man's strength had held her safe and warm. Almost like a cherished object. She shook her head. She was here to teach, not get addle-brained notions over a handsome man.

Standing, she reached to unhook the buttons on the back of her dress. She let it fall to the floor and hurriedly donned her thick nightgown against the room's chill. No matter how much she dwelled on the sheriff's nephews, she couldn't come up with a discipline she believed would cure them of their wild ways. She crawled under the quilts, and suddenly remembered what the Bible said about loving your enemies. She smiled.

But would overwhelming the boys with kindness work?

On the way home, Samson's hooves clopped against the hard ground, the sound bouncing back from the heavily wooded forest and pounding in Asher's skull. He'd most likely take sick from his romp in the woods. Not many men could ride all day in the cold, then venture out at night in freezing rain, giving up their coat, and expect not to take sick.

He shook his head. The little schoolmarm sure knew how to raise his hackles. And despite their challenging start, he'd meant to ask her if she'd watch the boys for a few days while he searched for their pa. Things on the mountain and down in the hollow seemed relatively quiet between the Joneses and the Sweeneys, at least for a fleeting moment. The hiring of a new teacher had raised his hopes that he'd actually have some time to search deeper for his brother. Even going as far south as Little Rock if the need arose.

He sighed. He certainly couldn't ask the spirited schoolmarm now. He'd have to leave the boys to their own devices and pray for the best. Matthew was twelve. Plenty old enough to look out for his brothers. Although he often led them straight into trouble. Asher would need to speak to him sternly. Something had to change.

He chuckled, envisioning how well a request for his nephews to stay under the same roof as the new teacher would go over. Like rain on a picnic, seeing how well they all got along. Pretty or not, the new schoolmarm was as prickly as a porcupine. Not that his nephews hadn't given her good reason to be. It was almost worth riling her to see her eyes flash the way they did when she got angry, or how her cheeks brightened when she tried to hold her tongue. If he had more time, Asher might enjoy getting to know her better. The hollow didn't make women like her. That was for sure.

Once he had the boys' futures in hand, their welfare taken care of, then he might have the luxury of courting a woman. But not now. Keeping the peace in Plumville and watching out for his nephews took all the time he had. Strangely enough, the thought left him feeling emptier and more lonesome than he could remember in a long time.

He dismounted in front of his cabin, thankful the sleet had stopped falling, and led Samson to the barn. While he brushed the wetness from his horse's coat, he couldn't get Charlotte's face out of his mind. What a feisty gal! He grinned. She'd need that kind of spunk to teach the children of this hollow.

With Samson cared for, Asher headed to the cabin. When he opened the door, three tousled heads peered down from the loft. He crossed his arms and narrowed his eyes. "What do the three of you have to say for yourself?"

"We were just funnin', Uncle Asher," Matthew stated. "We didn't mean any harm."

"Some pranks are dangerous. You could have hurt Miss Nelson. You need to think things through before acting on them." Asher plopped into his chair and tugged off his boots. "I'm thinking your actions warrant extra chores for the week. I'll leave a list on the table in the morning. Have you had supper?" They shook their heads. "Good. You can do without tonight."

"No trip to the woodshed?" Anticipatory tears welled in Mark's eyes.

"Have I ever swatted you boys?" A tickle started in Asher's throat and worked its way to his nose. He sneezed. Yep, he'd take sick for sure. The heaviness in his limbs and slight wheeze in his chest over the last few days wasn't weariness after all.

"No, sir. You're a right fine uncle," Matthew stated.

Maybe so, but he wasn't sure he was cut out to be a pa.

Chapter 5

Saturday morning, sun shining through a freshly washed window onto her scarred wood desk, Charlotte inserted her pen into the inkwell, thankful for a day to relax, write letters and plan studies. Spirits high with the warmer temperature, she tapped off the excess ink from her pen before setting it to paper.

Dear Mother and Father,

I have settled quite nicely into a cozy cabin in the quaint town of Plumville. The dishes came in quite handy as I hosted my first meal with the family of three of my students. Weather's been frightful with an unordinary cold front, but today's weather promises to be delightful.

Charlotte nibbled the end of her pen. She'd like to ask her mother for wisdom in handling the Thomas boys, but doing so would only convince her mother she'd been right in trying to keep Charlotte home and away from "hill people."

I have fifteen of the most enjoyable students. Two of the older ones fancy themselves in love. Isn't that endearing? I have enlisted the help of three boys to write the script to a Christmas play that I'm hoping will bring the town's citizens closer... Charlotte smiled, recalling the astonished looks on Matthew's, Mark's and Luke's faces.

Pounding on the door startled her, causing her to smear the previous word.

"Miss Nelson!"

Charlotte capped her ink and rushed to the door. Yanking it open, she came face-to-face with Matthew Thomas. "Matthew, what's wrong? What brings you out here so early?"

Tears shimmered in his eyes, yet the twelve-year-old squared his shoulders. "Uncle Asher is real sick. Me and my brothers don't know what to do for him, and we thought of you first thing. You being so smart and all."

Charlotte nodded. "Saddle Blue for me, please, and I'll get my bag. I've a few medicines that might help. Then hurry home and get some water boiling for tea." She held out a hand to stop him. "And plenty of blankets, all right?"

"Yes, ma'am. Blue's already ready. I reckoned you'd need him." Matthew leaped on the back of a brown mule and flapped his legs to encourage the animal to hurry. Seconds later, he'd disappeared in a cloud of dust.

The sheriff couldn't be sick from scouring the woods for her the day before, could he? No, illness didn't strike that quickly. She should have asked Matthew what his uncle's symptoms were. No help for it now. She would have to take her entire medical chest.

*Thank You, Lord, that Mother insisted we know how
to care for our servants when we had a plantation, and
that she insisted I bring an assortment of medicines
with me to Plumville.*

Charlotte pulled a black wooden chest from under
her bed, grabbed a lightweight shawl in case the day
grew colder later, then dashed out the front door. Blue
waited docilely next to the house. *Bless you, Matthew.*

After tying her chest behind the saddle, Charlotte
mounted and turned the mule toward the Thomas cabin.
She kicked and flicked the reins to no avail. Blue refused to go faster than a walk. Charlotte could have
made quicker progress on her own two feet.

What could be wrong with the sheriff? Not the last
two days of fishing her out of tough situations—outside
in punishing weather. Could it be influenza? Pneumonia? She racked her brain for remedies. How close was
the nearest doctor? She didn't recall seeing one when
she'd ridden past the mercantile, which made up the
"town," along with the church and school. She hadn't
even seen a sheriff's office. Asher must work out of
his home.

By the time she reached his cabin, the sun sat high
overhead and blazed with the intensity of an Indian
summer. Charlotte shook her head. Crazy, unpredictable
weather. She dismounted, untied her medicine chest,
then burst through the front door. "Matthew, take care
of Blue, please. Mark, is the water heated? Luke, fetch
me another quilt."

The boys scattered to do her bidding, Luke swiping
his arm across his eyes as he went. Charlotte knelt beside the cot where Asher lay and placed her hand on his
forehead. Mercy, he was hot. She'd brew some boneset
and wild cherry bark tea. Mark handed her the coffee-

pot of hot water. "Thank you. Now, I'll need a clean rag and a bowl of the coldest water you can find."

He raced away. When Matthew returned, Charlotte turned. "He's burning up with fever. Is there a doctor in Plumville?"

Matthew shook his head. "There's a yarb woman higher up the mountain. I can get her, if you want."

"An herb woman? No, not yet." Charlotte accepted the bowl of water from Mark and dipped a cotton rag in it. "I can do the same as she can. Come wipe your uncle's forehead while I make him some tea."

"Yes, ma'am."

Charlotte hurriedly mixed the tea. Asher's fever seemed dangerously high to her hands. She needed to listen to his lungs. But that would require removing his shirt. Her cheeks flamed at the thought. Maybe she could figure out a way without exposing too much skin.

Hoarse coughing drew her back to the cot. Charlotte withdrew a thick sheet of paper from her medicine box and rolled it into a tube. She eyed the buttons down the front of Asher's shirt. Maybe she could undo just a few, so she could fit the tube close to the skin.

Her fingers trembled as she unbuttoned the two top buttons. She raised her eyes to meet the worried gaze of Matthew. "Keep sponging his face while I listen to his lungs." She was thankful the three boys were present. They should be sufficient chaperonage if anyone posed questions about her being in a single man's home.

Asher's struggle to breathe was more evident as Charlotte placed one end of the tube to his chest and the other to her ear. His lungs wheezed and squeaked as he fought to draw in air. Her heart clenched to think the man had scoured the woods for her.

Tossing the paper tube into her medicine chest, Charlotte rushed to check the tea. She needed to break his fever, then she'd concentrate on his congested lungs. If only this out-of-the-way place had a doctor. Charlotte only knew the basics, whatever her mother had been able to drill into her head. But her skills weren't up to this. "Matthew, ride for the herb woman."

"He's sick bad?" Tears shimmered in the boy's eyes.

"I'm afraid so." Charlotte poured the tea into a mug. "Tell her he has a high fever and congested lungs. She'll know what to bring."

Matthew raced out the door while his brothers huddled around Charlotte. What could she say to relieve their fears? She'd seen people die before with the same symptoms. Well, she'd keep up a brave front and a smile on her face. She handed the bowl to Mark. "Could you get me some more cool water, please? Luke, you can hold your uncle's head while I spoon tea into his mouth."

Without opening his eyes, Asher gripped her hand, his heat all but searing her skin. "Don't let that old woman touch me."

Charlotte almost dropped the cup of tea. "You're... awake? That's good." Gracious. How did he feel about her unbuttoning his shirt? She placed her hand on his forehead. Still burning up.

"He means Miss Mahoney," Luke whispered. "Folks around here are afraid of her. Uncle told me once when he was little that he was sent to fetch her for his grandma, and the woman put leeches on her. She died."

"Then why in the world did I send for her?"

"She's the only doc we got in these parts, and Uncle is awful sick." Luke's chin quivered.

Charlotte nodded and dipped the spoon into the brew and willed her hand to stop shaking enough to spoon some between Asher's pale lips. "Drink this. It should help with the fever."

He opened his mouth then swallowed. "Tastes nasty."

"Yes, it does. Drink up like a good boy."

He pushed her hand away. "Don't spoon-feed me." With Luke's help, he lifted his head. "I'm not a baby."

Charlotte ducked her head to hide a smile. He might be sick, but he was definitely not a baby. Her gaze drifted to the muscled chest revealed through the top of his unbuttoned shirt. All man. She lifted the cup to his lips. "Try to drink all of it, if possible."

Before the drink was half-gone, Asher's eyes closed and his head fell back onto the pillow. Charlotte sighed. Where was the herb woman?

The little boy resumed mopping his uncle's forehead. "I don't want him to die."

Mark came inside and punched his brother in the shoulder. "He ain't gonna die."

"We don't hit each other." Charlotte slouched in her chair. High spots of scarlet colored Asher's cheeks, and perspiration plastered his hair to his head. She reached forward and smoothed a few strands away from his face.

When had she stopped thinking of him as Mr. Thomas? Was it when she'd ridden in front of him on his horse the day before?

She sighed, not being able to say for sure that he would live. But she prayed so, for the boys' sakes, and hers. Poor disciplinarian or not, she'd miss him if he passed. His square shoulders and flashing eyes.

"He's a better pa than Pa." Luke wiped his nose on his sleeve, causing Charlotte to cringe. "If he dies, who will take care of us?"

"We can take care of ourselves." Matthew burst

through the door. "Miss Mahoney's coming. Has to birth a baby first."

Heavens! That could take hours. And Asher's temperature could continue to rise. "Boys, I think you need to pray for your uncle."

"Yes, ma'am," they chorused and rushed to the table where all three folded their hands and bowed their heads.

Tears sprang to Charlotte's eyes, and she said her own prayer for Asher's healing before picking up the rag and wiping the perspiration from his forehead, his neck and past the collar of his shirt.

She needed to remain objective and pay no attention to the muscles beneath her hand, or the square jaw, or eyelashes longer than her own. If only the herb woman would arrive soon. With each swipe of the cloth, she prayed for healing, that Asher would hold on until the medicine woman got there, that Charlotte would know what to do.

Asher coughed, the sound harsh in the silent room, except for the crackling fire and the whispers of the boys' prayers. Charlotte tucked the blankets more firmly around him, hoping he'd sweat out his fever. "Matthew, do you have onions anywhere?"

"Yes, ma'am. A few."

"I need all you have to make a poultice." If she didn't break up the congestion in Asher's lungs, he'd have pneumonia for sure. Charlotte stood and dropped the rag into the bowl of water. "Mark, I need you and Luke to take over sponging your uncle."

The door banged open, and a breeze blew in a woman little over four feet tall and as wizened as an overripe apple. Charlotte clutched the neckline of her blouse and took a step back. The woman really was frightening!

"I'm Agnes Mahoney, and I'm here to fix the sheriff. You call me Agnes." She bustled to the cot and dropped a quilted bag on the floor. Loosening the drawstring around the top, she dug inside, the upper half of her body disappearing in the bag's depths.

Once Charlotte's heart rate returned to normal, she moved closer, intrigued by all the bottles and burlap pouches revealed.

Matthew grabbed her hand and leaned close to her ear. "Uncle Asher don't like the yarb woman. Don't let her do anything strange to him."

What constituted strange? Charlotte wasn't a doctor. Agnes looked ancient. Surely, she'd know whatever she needed to know.

"Promise, Teacher."

Charlotte took a deep breath. "I promise." Squaring her shoulders, she moved back to Asher's side. "I was getting ready to mix up an onion poultice. Would you like me to continue?"

Agnes straightened. "Can't hurt. I planned on using skunk oil, but I reckon iffen yous got some lobelia leaves to mix with the onion you can make up that poultice. I also got some wild plum bark that's been scraped down instead of up. Doesn't do to scrape it up, you know. You want the sickness to come out his feet, not settle up higher.

"I'll grind it and smoke it, blowing the smoke up under his shirt. That's bound to help with his breathing. What else you been doing for him?" The woman squinted, reminding Charlotte of a mole.

"I gave him some boneset and wild cherry bark tea." How in the world could smoke blown up his shirt help with his breathing? Was this one of the strange things she should keep the other woman from doing? And skunk oil? Gracious, they'd all stink to high heaven.

"And iffen y'alls got an animal to kill, I could use the blood. Good for lung troubles, you know, iffen the sick person drinks it fresh."

Absolutely not. Charlotte thrust out an arm to stop Matthew from darting outside to do the woman's bidding. "I'm afraid we're fresh out of animals to slaughter."

Agnes shrugged. "Guess I'll make do without."

"No skunk oil, either." Charlotte stood straight and lifted her chin.

Agnes peered at her. "You got some strange notions, girl. You want the sheriff to get better or not?"

"Of course I do." Charlotte resumed sponging Asher's face.

"Well, there's your problem." Agnes frowned. "The man's too clean what with you washing him. How long you been doing that?"

Lord, give me patience. "A couple of hours."

Agnes shook her head. "City folk sure are strange creatures." She tapped something into her pipe and lit it with an ember from the fireplace. "Hold up his shirt."

Asher struggled through darkness and heat to reach the light. Something weighed him down, and he thrashed against his captor. Ropes bound his legs, making it almost impossible to move. He fought his way to the surface.

Opening his eyes, he squinted against the glare of a lantern and tossed at least three quilts to the floor. Something that felt like whiskers brushed against his hand, and he turned his head. Ebony strands of hair tickled his hand. The schoolteacher's head lay on his cot. The fire's glow turned the ends of her hair blue. Most of the mass of curls fell out of the bun, cascading down Charlotte's back. His fingers inched closer, then froze.

What in the world was the teacher doing sleeping in his house? Where were the boys? He tried to sit, and Miss Nelson raised her head.

"Oh." She blinked, looking cuter than a beagle puppy. "You're awake." She laid a hand across his forehead, her skin cool and soft. "And fever free, praise the Lord."

"How long have I been sick?" Asher scooted to a sitting position and leaned against the wall behind his bed.

"You've been sleeping for three days." She stifled a yawn. "Excuse me."

"Then why aren't you at the school teaching? Where are the boys?"

"Your nephews are outside doing their chores. I canceled school the last two days. Now that you're better, it will resume tomorrow." She crossed her arms. "Don't look at me like that. Somebody had to watch over you."

He'd slept for three days? Impossible. Fragmented visions crossed his mind. "The old woman." He patted up and down his body. What had she done to him?

"No leeches or blood." Charlotte's shoulders sagged. Fatigue showed in every line of her body.

"Go home, Miss Nelson. I'll be fine now." Knowing that she'd stayed beside him, a virtual stranger she didn't see eye to eye with, was the best medicine he could receive. That and the fact she'd kept the herb woman from putting blood suckers all over him.

"I think I will." She stood and patted his shoulder. "Miss Mahoney a bad sort, Asher. She's an old woman who's set in her ways. She saved your life. I didn't have enough experience to doctor you." Her lips drew into a sad smile. "If not for her, I think you might have died." Grabbing her shawl from a hook by the door, Charlotte shuffled out, taking the day's sunshine with her.

She called him by his name. He liked the way it sounded coming from her, deep and throaty, and he planned on hearing her say his first name again as soon as he could finagle it from her. He touched the spot on his shoulder where she'd laid her hand. How long had it been since he'd had a comforting touch other than from one of the boys? Since his ma died over ten years ago, most likely.

"Uncle Asher's awake!" Luke wrapped his skinny little arms around Asher's neck. "We prayed bunches for you."

Matthew and Mark rushed to join them, grins splitting their faces. "You should've seen the schoolteacher, Uncle," Matthew stated. "Miss Mahoney wanted to make you drink blood, and Miss Nelson said no."

"She said it real mean, too, in that teacher voice of hers," Luke added. "Miss Mahoney said she had strange ideas, but I think she did the right thing, don't you?"

"I sure do." The thought of drinking fresh animal blood made him shudder. "Help me out of this bed." He planted the palms of his hands flat on the mattress and attempted to push to his feet.

"Uh-uh." Matthew shook his head. "Miss Nelson made us promise to keep you in bed for at least two more days."

"Well, Miss Nelson isn't here." He panted like a dog in the summer. Since when did the air get so thick? "What's wrong with me, anyway?"

"Pneumonia, best we can figure." Matthew wrapped a quilt around Asher's shoulders. "I reckon you can sit, but no standing. I don't want the teacher assigning us any more things to write. Boy, howdy, she's riled about you getting sick because you had to go looking for her. Made us copy the entire book of Luke."

Asher laughed, then almost coughed up a lung. The teacher was a spitfire for sure. He wished he would've been awake when she laid down the law and made them write. "Did y'all finish writing?"

Matthew shook his wrist. "Minutes ago. I think my hand is going to fall off."

"You deserved worse punishment, and you know it." Asher lay back on his bed. Maybe he wasn't ready to get up after all, but two more days in bed would drive him crazy.

He turned his head to see all three boys staring. "What?"

"Miss Nelson sure is pretty, ain't she?" Matthew asked.

"Yes, she is." Asher folded his arms behind his head.

"She's a mighty fine cook, too," Mark stated.

"Right fine."

"And she can take care of us boys real good, too," Luke said.

"Well, I reckon… Hey, what are you three up to?" Asher turned his head and speared them with a glance. Since when did his nephews list any teacher's attributes?

"Nothing. Just wanted you to know what a fine teacher she is." Matthew jerked his head toward the ladder leading to the loft. His brothers followed until all three were out of sight.

The rascals. They were up to something. If his head didn't hurt so much, he might be able to figure out what. As it was, he could do nothing more than to go back to sleep despite his guilt over the boys having to fend for themselves for another day. He was certain to be up and around by morning. How long could a man stay in bed, anyway?

Charlotte tucked her latest letter home into an envelope and left it in the center of the table, ready for her next trip to the mercantile. Which she hoped would be soon. She hadn't been back since the day they'd laughed at her and sent her scurrying. She'd have to swallow her pride and go back as soon as she made a poster announcing the pageant. She hoped they'd allow her to hang it in the front window.

Oh, what if she was the brunt of a joke again? She put her cool hands on her warm cheeks. Back home, no one laughed at the Nelsons. They were upstanding citizens, well respected within the community. Not one resident of Plumville had even bothered to stop by and welcome her to town. She needed to step out and visit them instead. But, oh, it would be cold traveling these hills this time of year. That's why she prayed the pageant would go well. So there'd be no need to brave the harsh weather in a hopeful attempt to get the citizens of Plumville to stop fighting with each other.

"Miss Nelson!" Matthew's voice rang through the door.

Charlotte rushed to let him inside. "What's wrong? Is your uncle all right?"

"No, ma'am." Matthew hung his head, a tear sliding down his freckled cheek. "He's doing right poorly, and I'm mighty worried."

"Let me get my cloak and my bag. Saddle up Blue for me, and we'll head right out."

The boy grinned and dashed out the door.

Charlotte stopped, frowning. Something didn't seem quite right. Yes, Matthew seemed genuinely worried about his uncle until she'd said they'd go. That would provide the boy some relief from his fears, but not enough to warrant a face-splitting grin.

Sighing, she grabbed her things, certain another practical joke loomed in her future. She prayed it wouldn't be one that would result in danger to herself or someone else. If Mother could see her now, traipsing through a cold winter day playing doctor to a man, she'd die of shock for sure. Charlotte laughed. It might do her mother's high-society spine a bit of good to loosen up with a prank or two, or some honest simple living.

True to his word, Matthew had Blue saddled and waiting for her. The boy was nowhere to be seen. No matter. Charlotte knew the way easily enough. She led the mule to a stump and, after securing her bag behind the saddle, swung up. With a flick of the reins, she set off toward the Thomas cabin.

The sun showed through the skeletal branches. Charlotte wished she could have seen the mountain in its fall finery. She'd heard tales of trees decked in colors of gold, crimson and pumpkin. She wasn't sure she'd see them next year, either. For her, Plumville was just the beginning. Maybe she could teach in Savannah, or perhaps a school in California. She grinned. Mother would have apoplexy if that should happen. She thought California was a den of iniquity.

Smoke rose through the trees ahead, signaling Charlotte's arrival at her destination. Mark waited out front, hopping from one foot to the other in an attempt to keep warm. Charlotte shook her head and handed him the reins to Blue. "You could have watched through the window. How's your uncle?"

"Right poorly." Mark hung his head. "I think he's dying, Miss Nelson."

Charlotte clutched the neck of her cloak. Heart in her throat, she shoved through the front door. She skidded to a halt.

Asher sat hunched over at the table, a hot cup of coffee in his hand, and a faded quilt around his shoulders. He peered at her with red-rimmed eyes. "Hey, Charlie."

"It's Charlotte." She shuddered at the dreaded nickname. "You look fine to me." A little weak, perhaps, but definitely not at death's door. She narrowed her eyes at the boys who scurried up the ladder to the loft.

"I've felt better, but doing all right. I appreciate your checking on me every day." Asher gestured to the seat across from him. "Sit and have a cup of coffee with me." He glanced at a clock on the mantel. "Already missed church. That's a shame."

Charlotte hadn't even realized until he spoke, and she'd so looked forward to her first church service in her new home, especially after having missed last week's services. "Guess we lost track of time with you being so ill. I seriously doubt, though, that you should have gone today, regardless of forgetting."

"Yeah, but it might have prevented those rascals upstairs from dragging you back over here." Asher smiled over the rim of his cup. "What did they tell you to get you to come running?"

"That you were dying." She chuckled.

"Yet you came." He wrapped the blanket tighter around his shoulders. "Despite our differences of opinion."

"Of course I would. I came last time you were ill, why not now?" Her face heated, realizing he was shirtless under the quilt. Heavens, she should leave and go home, but couldn't convince herself to leave the warmth of his fire to brave the cold just yet. "I'll even whip you up something to eat, if you'd like."

"That won't be needed, thank you. My main concern is the ongoing feud. With me laid up in bed, I can't be riding the mountain, keeping an eye on things."

Well, Charlotte still hadn't visited the families of her pupils. She could do one family a night, although before she finished, Asher would be back on his horse. "I could ask around the mercantile to see whether there is anything pressing for your attention."

"I don't want you to go to any trouble." Asher drained the last of his coffee. "Thank you for stopping by, but I'm thinking it's best if I go lie down." The corner of his mouth quirked. "You do realize the boys have set their eye on you as my future wife, right? That's why they fetched you today."

Gracious. The breath left Charlotte. An act of good-will might have stopped the pranks and started something a whole lot worse.

Chapter 6

Charlotte stared over the heads of her students, waiting while they took their seats and settled down. It was October, and they needed to get started on the Christmas play if everything was going to run smoothly. Once all eyes looked her way, she welcomed the class and got straight to business. "Lucy, Frank, I would like the two of you to play Mary and Joseph in our pageant. One of your infant brothers or sisters can play the part of the baby Jesus."

Lucy squealed and tossed a grin at Frank who winked. Then, as if someone dumped a bucket of snow on a fire, Lucy's smile faded. "My pa won't let me. Not if Frank is in it, too. Especially not if we're to be Mary and Joseph."

"Well, of course, all the students will be in the pageant. Surely your parents will understand?"

Every head except for the three Thomas boys, and

one or two others from families not involved in the feud, shook from side to side.

"None of your parents will allow it?" This could not be possible. "I suppose I'll have to speak with all of them." One way or the other, she would make this town see reason.

"You can speak to my pa at church," Lucy said. "He's the preacher man."

Really? "And yet your father is involved in a feud?" An inconceivable thought to Charlotte.

"Well, he didn't start it, ma'am." Lucy's brow wrinkled. "It's just been happening since Moses parted the Red Sea, most likely."

"For goodness' sake." Charlotte plopped into her chair. This would not do at all. Did anyone in Plumville even know what they were feuding about? How could a man of God show favoritism amongst his congregation? Or maybe he left that particular sin for every day except Sunday.

Taking a deep breath, she got to her feet. "I'll take care of everything, and the play will proceed as planned. The Thomas boys will be the three wise men. The rest of you will be our choir of angels and shepherds." Charlotte forced a smile to her trembling lips.

"I'm asking each of you to write something to be read during our celebration." Multiple groans arose. "It can be a poem, a story, or a favorite Christmas memory. I will assist the younger students. The script for the play will be written by the Thomas boys."

The three boys put their heads on their desks, proving to be great actors with their dramatic action. Luke raised his hand. "I can't hardly spell my name. How am I supposed to write a play?"

"You spell fine," Charlotte told him. "No amount of

excuses will get you boys out of this. This is penance for locking me in the outhouse."

A chorus of laughter rang out.

She narrowed her eyes until she regained control of the class. "If the three of you pull any more shenanigans, I'll have you sing a song, too."

"That ain't fair." Matthew bolted to his feet. "Since you saved our uncle, we thought you'd be nice to us."

"I am very nice. Now, I'd like you all to pull out your slates and copy your spelling words from the board." Charlotte jimmied open her one and only desk drawer, which took quite a bit of effort, and pulled out her roll book. When she opened it, a piece of torn paper fluttered to her desk. She flipped it over and read, "Wil u mary me? Ascher Thomas."

Gracious. She put her hands to her flaming cheeks then speared the Thomas boys with a stern glance. She crooked her finger at Matthew, motioning for him to approach her. When he did, she tapped her pencil on the note and lowered her voice to little more than a whisper. "Did you write this?"

"No, ma'am." His neck reddened.

"Well, I know your uncle didn't write it." Surely, the sheriff could spell his own name.

"Mark did."

"At your encouragement?"

"Maybe." He scuffed his foot on the floor. "You'd make him a good wife, Miss Nelson."

"Thank you, but whom I choose to marry is not your concern." She stood and moved to the front of the desk. With her finger under his chin, she tilted his face to look at her. "Teachers cannot marry, Matthew, but I appreciate the gesture."

His eyes widened. "They can't?"

"No, sir." She fought to control her smile. "When, and if, a teacher marries, she has to stop teaching. A woman's place is in the home, caring for her husband and children. Since I love teaching, marriage and a family are not in my foreseeable future."

"Oh." He frowned for a moment, then grinned. "All right." The boy dashed back to his seat.

What had she told him to warrant such a response? She feared that, instead of discouraging him, she might have unknowingly lit a fire under his backside. Sighing, she returned to taking roll.

What would it be like to be married to Asher Thomas? Why hadn't the man taken a wife yet? He was certainly handsome enough. Surely, the mountain was full of eligible girls more than willing to settle down. Just not Charlotte. Maybe someday, if she could find a man willing to overlook her stubborn ways and sharp tongue. Mother said no man alive would do so, and that Charlotte needed to learn to be more womanly in order to marry. Should the time come when Charlotte set her eyes on someone, the man would have to accept her as she was or not at all.

She slapped the book closed and erased the spelling words. If she continued to dwell on her own thoughts, the students would learn nothing, and she would have failed as their teacher.

"I know one of those Sweeneys left my gate open, Sheriff." Hank pointed at a carcass, its stomach cavity mangled, its brown-and-white winter fur spotted with blood. "Now, a wolf has killed a prize heifer. I demand you do something."

"I will." Asher clenched his teeth in an effort not to berate the fool. "Last time you blamed something on the Sweeneys, it was one of your own children that was negligent. Perhaps it's the same thing here." After all, the man had six young'uns. His poor wife couldn't keep track of all of them every second of the day.

"Whose side are you on?" Hank balled his fists and planted them on his hips. "We need an impartial sheriff in these parts."

"I am impartial, and I will talk to Duke Sweeney. I'm only saying you shouldn't be so quick to make judgment."

"And you should be quicker to make an arrest!" Hank kicked a rock, sending it into the side of his barn.

"I'll let you know what he says." Asher marched to his horse and swung into the saddle.

Going to question Duke was a waste of time. The man had better things to do than let someone else's cow out of the winter pasture. If the man wanted to do harm, a bullet would work better. If not for the stupid feud, there'd be little to no crime in Plumville, and Asher would have more time to search for his no-account brother.

The two men who once fought over a girl decades ago were long dead. The lady hadn't married either one of them, instead, choosing to marry a city fella and move away. Yet the feud remained, carried on by hardheaded kinfolk.

After pulling the collar of his coat up around his neck, Asher guided his horse along the path leading to the opposite side of the mountain. Because of the feud, the families wanted as much distance between homesteads as possible, eating up most of Asher's day every time he had to ride back and forth, not to mention their own long travels to attend church and send their children to school.

Asher coughed and shrugged down into his wool-lined leather coat. They might not have had any more snow, but the wind could cut a man in half. He smiled, imagining Miss Nelson's face if she found out he was riding in the cold so soon after his illness.

An hour later, he arrived at Duke Sweeney's run-down cabin. Two mangy dogs, too lazy to even bark, looked up at him from their spot on the lopsided porch. If Duke had left a gate open, he would have stolen the cow to eat, not left it to the wolves.

But Asher had a job to do. He draped his horse's reins over a porch rail and knocked on Duke's door.

"Hold on! You better not be selling anything," Duke hollered.

Who would come all this way to sell something? Asher removed his hat and waited. "It's the sheriff."

"I ain't done nothin'!"

"Just come on out and talk to me for a minute."

Instead, the man sent his very pregnant wife to open the door. "Come on in, Sheriff. Want a cup of coffee?"

"No, thank you, Daisy Mae, I'm here on business."

"For my husband or one of the young'uns?"

"I'm just asking some questions." Asher stepped into the dim, chilly room.

Duke glanced up from a bowl of soup. "What can I do for you? Y'all eat." He pointed his spoon at his three children. "Your ma worked hard. Wife, I need some more coffee."

Asher had a feeling the soup would be cold by the time Daisy Mae sat down to eat. "Know anything about Hank's cows getting out?"

"Nope." He dug back into his meal.

"You sure?"

"Sheriff, if you're accusing me of something come right out and say so." Duke lumbered to his feet. "Why would I go to the other side of this hill just to open someone's gate? I would have at least let all the cows out and taken one. How many are missing?"

"Just one, and it's not really missing." Asher ran his fingers through his hair, knowing the action would have his curls sticking out everywhere. "And a wolf got it."

"Well, there you go. A wolf left that gate open." Duke laughed so hard soup dribbled down his chin. "Sheriff, you're a riot. A regular riot. You're almost as bad as that teacher who wants to have a play with all the young'uns in it. A mighty big undertaking."

"Yes, it is. You going to let yours participate?"

"Maybe." Duke rubbed his belly. "Might be interesting. But I doubt Hank is going to let his boy be Joseph to Lucy's Mary, if you know what I mean. Uh-huh. If I were you, Sheriff, instead of bothering folks who mind their own business, I'd focus on wooing that pretty little teacher and hitching your wagon up to hers. Might get her off everyone else's back."

"I'm not looking to get married." Asher nodded at Daisy Mae and headed for the door. "Y'all have a good evening."

"Ain't what the children from that school are saying." Hank guffawed. "Heard tell just today that the teacher got herself a proposal letter from you."

"What are you saying?" Blood rushed to Asher's feet.

"She got a note that said you wanted to marry her."

Asher's steps faltered, then he ran as if the hounds of Hades were on his heels. If he found out those nephews of his were spouting words of nonsense to Miss Nelson, he'd tan them for sure. How would he face the teacher again? He'd never be able to look her in the eyes.

Marry the new teacher? Him? Not likely. He barely had time to breathe. Saints alive, the woman had seen him at his worst—and shirtless. Sweat beaded on his brow. He'd never live down the humiliation.

Charlotte stepped into the general store and took a deep breath. The scents of wood smoke and cinnamon greeted her, and she smiled, soaking in the wonderful aromas of the approaching holidays. Thanksgiving, then Christmas. The shining point would be the Christmas play. The one thing that could take her mind off the fact she would spend the holidays alone this year.

"Good morning, Mrs. Mabry." Charlotte strolled to the counter. "I have a letter to mail and am also wondering whether I might be able to post an advertisement in your window informing folks about our upcoming Christmas pageant."

"Of course, dear, it's all everyone is talking about." The store owner came around the front of the counter.

"Really?" Warmth flooded Charlotte. "They're excited?"

"Not necessarily." Mrs. Mabry took the flyer and stuck it in the window. "Some are fuming, others are laughing. There are very few folks in this town who remain impartial to an age-old grievance between families." She turned with a smile. "But don't worry your pretty head. They'll come around."

"I hope so." Charlotte handed her the envelope. "I also need the items from this list, please."

What would she do if no one showed up or participated in the play? Her first undertaking as a teacher would be a failure. Everyone back home would say "I told you so."

Charlotte almost stamped her foot. She wouldn't give

them the satisfaction. Her plan had to work. The children were the first step. Convince them, then the parents would follow. Then, even the toughest naysayer would be convinced to set aside their differences.

The bell over the door jingled. Charlotte turned as Asher entered and headed straight for the stove. The boys followed close on his heels.

"It's colder than a boar hog's—" Matthew sidled next to his uncle.

Asher narrowed his eyes. "Finish that sentence and you won't be able to sit for a month."

Charlotte put a gloved hand over her mouth to hide a smile. The sheriff definitely had his hands full. Thank goodness he seemed to be undertaking a more active role in his nephews' discipline. "Good afternoon, Sheriff."

"Miss Nelson." Asher nodded. "I thought I recognized Blue. I hope my nephews have been behaving themselves at school." He raised an eyebrow in question.

Did he know about the note? "Much better." Charlotte gulped, and whirled back to the counter. Bracing her hands on the smooth wood top, she struggled to catch her breath. How could she face him if he knew?

"Are you all right, Miss Nelson?" Asher moved to her side, bending to peer into her face. "You look flushed. You aren't taking ill, are you?"

His proximity wasn't helping a bit. "No, it's just the heat of the store. I'll be fine once I step outside."

"She brung us a flyer about the play," Mrs. Mabry stated, pointing at the window. "I think she's got herself in a dither that folks might not come."

"No, that isn't it." Gracious, what could she say without letting Asher know how much he affected her? "God will bring the people to the play, and thank you, Mr. Thomas, but I don't believe I'm taking ill. I've allowed myself to become overly warm, that's all. Good day." She marched out the door.

"Miss Nelson!"

Charlotte froze and closed her eyes. She'd walked out and forgotten her purchases. Oh, that man did fluster her. She needed to devise a way to keep clear of him or she'd lose her mind. She turned and reentered the store, grabbing her package from the sheriff's hands. "Thank you."

"Miss Nelson," Mrs. Mabry called after her when Charlotte again headed for the door. "Do you want me to put those on your credit?"

"Yes, please." Never in her life had Charlotte charged anything, but she could not go back in the store. Not with Asher's gaze resting on her like hot coals, or the way he smelled. Heavens, but the man smelled like smoke, fresh air, pine and something all him that mixed together wreaked havoc on her senses.

After tying her package behind the mule's saddle, Charlotte led the animal to a stump and hefted herself into the saddle. Once, her father had owned several fine riding horses, but they'd been sold during the war. Blue might not be as pretty as those horses, but he beat walking. Charlotte pointed him toward home.

The clip-clop of his hooves lulled her into a peace mimicked by the soft breeze through the trees. A cardinal landed in a pine tree, the vibrant scarlet of its feathers a pleasing contrast to the tree's green. With God's glory all around her, and a job she loved, Charlotte had many things to thank God for. Which turned her mind to Thanksgiving. Where would she spend that wonderful day this year? Maybe the family of one of her students would issue an invitation.

Oh, no. What if an invitation came from the Thomas household?

"That gal might be pretty, but she needs to get her head out of the clouds," Mrs. Mabry stated as she handed Asher a sack of flour. "Dizziest girl I've seen in a long time. City folk are strange creatures, aren't they?"

"Just got a lot on her mind, I'm sure." Asher handed the bag to Matthew, then grabbed peppermint sticks for the boys from a jar on the counter. "She's got a school full of students, she's new to town, and now she's trying to put together that play." And she could be flustered because she thought Asher had proposed marriage to her.

The thought chilled his blood. Get married? Not likely, but then if the little gal said no, it might hurt his feelings. Why wouldn't a woman want to get hitched with him? He had a steady job, a sturdy home, everything a man needed to make a woman happy. He was as bad as Miss Nelson, walking around without his feet firmly planted on the ground. He'd always prided himself on being a level-headed man. Now a little slip of a woman managed to turn his world upside down.

Somehow, he had to find out what was going through the pretty teacher's head. If she was planning a wedding announcement, Asher was in a heap of trouble. He glanced at the flyer in the window to make sure she hadn't said anything on there. Nope, just about the play. That ought to create a riot.

"Come on, boys." Asher grabbed a box of jarred vegetables that Mrs. Mabry always put up for him. "Help me carry and let's get home to eat." They'd have something easy, like eggs and bacon, but at least the boys would have food in their bellies. Maybe he should think more seriously about settling down.

What if he never found his brother and was responsible for his nephews for an indefinite amount of time? They'd need a mother figure. Someone who could help keep them in line, yet nurture and love them. Someone like Miss Nelson. No! He shook his head to rid it of troublesome thoughts. He'd manage on his own. He definitely didn't need an opinionated woman, no matter how comely she was or how good of a nurse.

By the time he pulled himself out of his daydreams, the boys had gathered around the flyer.

"I don't wanna write that stupid play," Mark whined. "Too much work. It was your fault we locked the teacher in the outhouse. You should write it yourself." He punched Matthew in the arm.

"Yeah!" Luke punched him in the other one. "You're always getting us in trouble."

"Boys." Asher stepped up behind them and read the flyer over their heads.

Citizens of Plumville are invited to attend a Christmas pageant on Christmas Eve. The students of Plumville's school will perform, sing and read their special writings. Come be entertained and blessed.

Miss Nelson had even drawn a crude Christmas tree in the bottom corner of the flyer. Well, Asher supposed some folks would show up, out of curiosity if nothing else. The Thomas family, at least, would be there. Mrs. Mabry and her husband, no doubt.

The first Sunday that Miss Nelson attended church, she'd see how it was. She'd take note of the Sweeney side and the Jones side. Asher and the boys usually stood in the back, as close to the door as possible in order not to have one side believe they sided over the other. On days when Pastor Sweeney was long-winded, Asher was almost tempted to take the Sweeney side just to sit down. It'd be interesting to see how the teacher handled the situation.

He put the supplies in the back of the wagon. "Come on, boys. It's going to be dark soon."

They scampered to do his bidding as Asher climbed into the driver's seat and released the brake. His breath plumed in front of him. Not even Thanksgiving yet, and the cold was enough to chill your bones.

Most likely, they'd spend that particular holiday with the Widow Slater, same as last year. The only problem was, Asher got the feeling the woman was putting her brand on him. They got some funny smirks at social gatherings.

He flicked the reins, sending the horses plodding forward. Only a few years older than Asher, the widow still looked mighty fine as far as wife material went, and no amount of rejecting her advances convinced her that Asher didn't want to get married. No, maybe they'd stay home this year. The boys would get over their disappointment at not having a meal with all the fixings, but it would be worth it in the end.

"Whoa." He pulled back on the reins. A few yards ahead, Miss Nelson kicked her heels frantically against the mule's sides. Asher stopped the wagon beside her, reached over and slapped Blue's rump, sending the mule jumping sideways and then taking off at a dead run.

"Thank you!" Miss Nelson called over her shoulder. Her hat blew off and landed on a bush. "Could you fetch that, please? I'm afraid both hands are occupied right now." Asher laughed and set the wagon back into motion. Matthew grabbed the hat as they passed and waved it over his head, yelling like a banshee. The noise only made Blue kick up his heels and bray. If the animal didn't settle down, Miss Nelson would find herself in a ditch.

Flicking the reins, Asher urged his horses faster and rejoiced as the wagon drew near to the teacher. The whites of the mule's eyes shone as the animal skittered sideways.

"Pull back!" Asher reached out to grab the mule's bridle. His arms were a few inches too short. "Lean closer."

"What?" Her eyes widened. "Are you crazy?"

"Lean over, and I'll pull you to the wagon."

"You'll get us both killed." She tugged harder, the bit biting into the mule's soft mouth. The mule stopped and kicked.

"You're hurting the mule." Maybe Asher could appeal to her soft nature. "He won't settle down now until you're off him, and he is determined to get you off, one way or the other."

"Oh." She let go and held out her arms like a baby reaching for her daddy.

Asher grabbed her under the armpits and dragged her over, dumping her onto his lap and knocking the breath out of himself. Boy, she sure smelled pretty and felt so soft and warm.

Chapter 7

Charlotte straightened the small wool hat on her head and paused in the doorway to the sanctuary. Predominantly blond-haired people filled one side, dark-haired the other. Clearly the line between Jones and Sweeney was drawn, even at church. Which side should an impartial churchgoer take?

Where did the Mabrys sit? Charlotte craned her neck, not catching a glimpse of the shop owner. Maybe the woman and her husband didn't attend church. She then searched for the Thomases. No sign of them, either. Now she was in a pickle. She could choose a seat in the back row, but even then she had to sit on a particular side.

She clenched her fists, the fabric of her gloves rasping together. Multiple heads turned. Gazes fixed on her with glares and questions. Mercy. She turned to flee, only to find herself nose to chest with Asher.

"We usually stand in the back." He took her elbow and guided her right inside the door. "It's uncomfortable, but easier."

"Oh, dear." Already Charlotte's feet hurt in the tight fashionable boots she'd insisted on bringing with her from Savannah. Horribly impractical for teaching, but she'd thought they'd be suitable for church. Resigned, she leaned against the back wall and shifted from foot to foot, trying to banish the pinching of her toes, and feeling every bit like a naughty schoolgirl sent to stand in the back of the room as discipline.

"Just pray Pastor Sweeney isn't long-winded." Asher's whisper tickled the short curls beside Charlotte's ear, almost making her forget about her feet.

"Do you stand every week?" Charlotte found it hard to believe that the sheriff would allow the townspeople to dictate his comfort during church service. "Maybe you should build your own pew."

"Would you share it with me?" His eyes twinkled.

Heavens. Charlotte clutched the lace around her throat and ducked her head to hide her flaming cheeks. A woman in the row in front of them turned around and glared, putting a bony finger against her lips. Another woman, a lovely blonde with a peaches-and-cream complexion, glanced past Charlotte and smiled at Asher, inclining her head in invitation. He shook his head.

Charlotte sighed and prepared herself to endure the morning. Maybe the sermon would be riveting enough to keep her concentration.

"Save my spot." Asher squeezed past her. "I'll be back in a minute." He moved toward where Luke crawled under a pew after an errant ball. As the congregation stood to sing a hymn, he ushered his youngest nephew out the sanctuary door.

Charlotte gave him a nod, inwardly pleased that he intended to speak with the boy about crawling on the floor during church. Luke wasn't an infant, after all. When Asher hadn't returned by the time the song was over, she stood on her tiptoes and glanced out the small window in the door.

Uncle and nephew tossed a ball back and forth a few times, then Asher handed it to Luke and clapped the boy on the shoulder before heading back toward the building. Charlotte quickly got back to her spot. Really? He took Luke outside to play? What kind of a guardian was Asher Thomas? Charlotte gnawed her lower lip. Should she speak to the man or leave things alone? Unless the boy's behavior directly concerned her, she should keep her thoughts to herself, correct? Her heart fell as her esteem for the sheriff dropped.

"Had something I needed to take care of." He flashed her a grin before sliding back into place.

Charlotte lifted her chin, choosing to ignore him, and instead focused on the short man approaching the pulpit. Pastor Sweeney might be taller than Charlotte by an inch or two, if that. The man in no way resembled his fair, lovely daughter, Lucy, except for the hair. A large nose was prominent under eyes magnified behind his spectacle lenses. Poor man. He must have been teased unmercifully during his childhood.

His high-pitched voice squeaked out a sermon on counting one's blessings during the Thanksgiving holiday, something Charlotte definitely agreed with. But the way the man's face turned red, and sweat beaded on his brow as he tried to hammer across the fact that God expected them to be thankful over everything, left a giggle bubbling inside of her. It released in a snort, gaining her another indignant look from the woman in the row in front of her.

"I'm sorry," Charlotte mouthed. Oh, how could she? Her first Sunday attendance, and she was no better than Luke had been.

"Let's close today's service with 'Amazing Grace.'" Pastor Sweeney stepped back and let a plump woman take his place.

As soon as she opened her mouth to sing, the congregation joined in. Asher opened his mouth and let loose a rich baritone, as pure and fluid as a mountain stream.

Charlotte clamped her mouth shut, closed her eyes and listened, feeling as if she were in front of God's throne listening to an angel. She simply must have him sing at the play. Immediately upon dismissal, she'd ask him. Surely the man knew the quality of his singing and would be more than happy to help her.

By the time Pastor Sweeney said his closing prayer, Charlotte's toes were numb and the bottoms of her feet felt bruised. Still, she allowed Asher to escort her to the receiving line to meet the pastor. "You have a beautiful voice, Asher."

"Thank you, ma'am." He placed his hand on the small of her back and guided her forward.

She smiled over her shoulder. "I'd like you to use the gift God gave you and sing a solo during the Christmas pageant."

Was she mad? Asher stumbled. Instead of offering his hand to Pastor Sweeney, he slammed into the man's shoulder. Asher had sometimes wondered if the new teacher was a mite touched in the head. Now he knew for certain she was. Him, sing in front of a group of people? Not likely.

He regained his footing. "Excuse me, Pastor, didn't mean to knock into you like that."

"Apology accepted." He grinned at Charlotte. "You must be the new schoolteacher. Lucy has said many nice things about you. I hope you enjoyed today's sermon."

Charlotte offered him a gloved hand. "Really? That's perfect because—"

"Have a nice afternoon, Pastor." Asher rushed Charlotte outside and past the lovely blonde woman who started to approach them. "Don't start every conversation with the play." He turned her to face him. "Do you want to start a riot? It's obvious Pastor Sweeney has no idea what you've asked his daughter to do. It's best you leave it until she can convince him or the man knows you better."

Charlotte pulled free of his grasp. "This is ridiculous. Having to stand up in church for fear of choosing sides. The pastor possibly reluctant to allow his child to be in a *Christmas* play. My feet haven't hurt like this in ages. Why, the very idea would have my mother in fits. Church should be a place of neutrality."

"Yes, but this one isn't." He cupped her elbow and led her to a bench. "Forcing folks around here to do something they don't want to do can get a person hurt."

She set her reticule in her lap. "How do they know they don't want to do it if they haven't tried? Has anyone done any kind of program here before that would draw folks together?" When he shook his head, she continued, "This town needs to come together in some way, and the school program is the perfect solution." She straightened her shoulders and pierced him with eyes the color of a stormy winter sky. "I don't intend to back down, Mr. Thomas. As much as Pastor Sweeney's voice sounds like nails on a chalkboard, I intend to ask him to be a narrator in the play. That will be one more way to bring this town closer together."

"It isn't up to you to bring this town together." Asher crossed his arms. "It also isn't up to me. I'm here to keep the law, nothing more. You're here to teach the children."

Charlotte lunged to her feet, high spots of color on her cheekbones. "Maybe that's what's wrong with this town!"

He bent until their noses were almost touching. "Pardon me?"

"If you are as lax with the people of this town as you are with your nephews, it's no wonder they're so divided." She clapped a hand over her mouth. "I'm so sorry. I shouldn't have said anything."

"Are you referring to me taking Luke outside and tossing a ball around during church?" How dare she judge him? "It was the ball of a little boy a few rows ahead of us. He needed his ball restrung. Luke wanted to help the child, so we restrung it then tossed it back and forth a couple of times to make sure it would suffice for play." Why was he explaining himself to a sharp-tongued woman who meddled in other people's affairs?

"Oh, well, I didn't—"

"No, ma'am, you didn't." Asher turned to leave, coming face-to-face with the pastor and the Widow Slater.

"Mr. Thomas, Miss Nelson, is everything all right?" The pastor folded his hands in front of his waist. "Your voices are growing quite loud, and since this is a house of God, I felt led to interrupt what seemed to be a rather heated conversation."

Charlotte drew breath sharply through her nose. "Just a misunderstanding, sir. But now that you are here—"

"Pastor!" Hank Jones stood at the bottom of the church steps. "A word, if you please."

"Excuse me, Miss Nelson. We'll continue this conversation later, tomorrow at the latest." He rushed away.

"I need to go, too, and make sure they don't start fighting." Asher tightened his hat on his head. "Miss Nelson, this is the Widow Slater."

"Nice to meet you, Mrs. Slater." Charlotte waved a hand at Asher. "Of course, go. It's a wonder anything gets done around here, let alone finish a conversation."

Oh, they'd finish their conversation all right. As soon as Asher finished with the current crisis.

"Don't forget about singing in the play, Mr. Thomas." Her words followed him. He'd meant to tell her she was asking the impossible. God might have bestowed the gift of song on Asher, but standing in front of a group of people and using it? No, not happening.

He'd tried the group thing once in school, when the teacher had instructed the class to read a page from their primers out loud. When Asher stumbled over a couple of the more difficult words, the class had laughed. He'd never stood in front of a crowd again.

"You owe me a cow!" Hank poked his forefinger in the pastor's chest. "If your no-good brother didn't leave my gate open, then it had to be you or your wanton daughter."

"My Lucy is as pure as an angel!" Pastor Sweeney two-hand shoved Hank. "I don't know anything about your cow or your gate."

Asher stepped between the two. "Gentlemen, please remember where you are. Hank, I told you I would take care of this. Pastor, you're a man of God. This is not proper behavior for either one of you."

"But he insulted my Lucy." Pastor Sweeney crossed his arms and glared.

"Everybody knows she's making eyes at my Frank."

"It's the other way around." Sweeney took a step forward.

Asher planted a palm on each man's chest and gave them a push. "That's enough. We don't insult each other's children, nor do we throw punches in the churchyard. If you don't break it up, I'll have to haul the both of you to jail for the night."

"We don't have a jail," Hank stated.

"But I got a shed that works as such if we need it." Asher really needed to build a proper jail. After he figured out how to tell the teacher he wouldn't sing in her program.

Asher sank the ax head into the wood, enjoying the feel of working muscles, knowing that his endeavors would keep his family warm during the winter. And the physical labor allowed him to work off some of his frustration with the starry-eyed new teacher.

Pastor Sweeney had ridden by announcing that he was on his way to pay a call to the "lovely Miss Nelson" and to invite her to dinner. Asher couldn't be jealous, could he? After all, Charlotte wanted the pastor to narrate the play, nothing more. Pastor Sweeney might have ideas in his head, but the feisty schoolteacher would have ideas of her own.

In Asher's opinion, she ought to stick to teaching reading, writing and arithmetic. It was no small feat, considering she had a schoolroom full of Joneses and Sweeneys that fought as often as their parents did. That should keep her hands more than full and not allow a lot of time for nonsense such as a school play.

He snorted. Him, sing in public? Ha. He swung the ax with a resounding thump.

Sweat trickled down his back despite the wintry chill and his lack of a coat. If he kept chopping at the rate he was working, he'd have enough wood to share with the widow and the teacher.

"You act like you're going to kill that wood, Uncle Asher." Matthew grabbed another armload to carry over to the wood pile. "Why are we working on a Sunday, anyway? We're not supposed to work on a Sunday, according to the Widow Slater. It's almost suppertime, and we're hungry. The widow sent over stew, and the smell's making my stomach growl."

Asher sighed at Matthew's rambling dramatics and the widow's unwillingness to stop acting like she and Asher were courting. "You can leave the wood until tomorrow. I'm just working off steam." *Thunk.*

"Whose head you trying to chop off? The teacher's or the widow's?"

Neither. Both. Obviously, he wasn't setting a very good example for his nephew. His brother always did say that everything Asher felt or thought showed on his face. "Nah, Miss Nelson wants me to sing in the play."

"You gonna?" Matthew dumped his armload, missing the pile by a foot. One piece rolled to a stop near Asher's foot.

"Nope." Asher swung the ax. *Thunk.* "Can't abide performing in public." *Thunk.*

"Yippee! Now we ain't going to, either." Matthew darted away.

Nothing like unraveling something before a project even got started. Miss Nelson would have his head on the chopping block. He needed to figure a way out of the mess he'd made. The boys could not back out of performing. Asher didn't want to see the shadow of hurt cloud Charlotte's blue eyes for a second time.

The sound of a horse's hooves drew Charlotte to the window. She parted the gingham curtains she'd hung the week before and watched as Pastor Sweeney dismounted and sauntered toward her door. The man definitely stayed true to his word. He'd said he'd see her later and here he was, visiting the very same day. She'd expected him to visit later in the week.

Charlotte grabbed her shawl, draped it around her shoulders, then stepped outside. "Pastor, thank you for coming."

"My pleasure, Miss Nelson." He removed his black felt hat. "You had something you wished to discuss with me? I'm terribly sorry about being pulled away from you so abruptly, but a pastor's work is never done. May we step inside, out of the cold?"

"Oh, no, that wouldn't be proper." Although, the wind did carry a stinging bite. Charlotte pulled her shawl tighter. "I'll make my request brief. As you know, I'm working with the students of Plumville to present a Christmas pageant. You would make the perfect narrator."

His eyebrows rose. "Well, I'm flattered, but not sure I should partake in a play that will also have Jones children."

"Sir—" Charlotte stiffened "—as a man of God you should be above such petty differences."

"As I strive to do on Sundays, but I am only human, Miss Nelson, and fall prey to the same temptations as other men."

"You must pull yourself above such things, Pastor Sweeney, if you hope to shepherd your flock effectively." Charlotte shivered, wishing the man would hurry and give her an answer so she could escape to the warmth of her fire. "I also believe that Lucy will make the perfect Mary. She is a beautiful girl."

His thin lips spread in a smile. "Not only beautiful, but wise. Please be our guest at supper tomorrow night, and we will discuss this further. Good day, Miss Nelson."

"Good day, Pastor Sweeney, and I accept your invitation."

Turning, he replaced his hat on his head and lifted his left foot into the horse's stirrup. "Wonderful. We look forward to sampling your cooking. I'm sure Lucy will be very happy to have another woman in her life."

"What?" Charlotte's mouth fell open as the man rode away. He had the audacity to invite her over for dinner then tell her she would do the cooking? Another woman in his daughter's life? No, she must have heard him wrong. No sooner had she turned for her door, than more hooves sounded. She shivered again and waited while Asher dismounted. Goodness, her little plot of land was busy this evening.

"Charlotte." Asher tipped his hat.

"Asher." She lifted her chin. "Have you arrived to tell me you'll be happy to sing in my program?"

"No, ma'am." He approached, twisting the brim of his hat. "Nothing quite as glad as that. I've come to tell you that through my own senseless actions, the boys are now refusing to be in the play."

She narrowed her eyes and peered into his face. Remorse and embarrassment colored his cheeks. "Then you must agree to sing so they *will* perform."

"I can't. It's fine in a group when no one is looking at me, but alone, I'll freeze up and make a fool of myself." He shook his head. "No, we'll have to think of something else."

"There is nothing else." Tears stung her throat. How could he be so cruel? "Everything is falling apart."

"What about Sweeney?"

She shrugged. "He wants me to come over for dinner tomorrow night to discuss the play and his and his daughter's role in it. He actually asked me to prepare the food. Is that a normal custom in the hollow? To ask the guest to bring the meal?"

Asher chuckled. "No, that means he's got his eye on you for a possible wife, and he's testing your cooking."

"A wife? Then I'll burn the food on purpose." There must be a mistake. She'd done nothing to lead the pastor into believing she felt any attraction toward him. It was better she focus on the play and not these hill people's strange notions. "As the boys' uncle, it is your duty to convince them to fulfill their word to act as the three wise men."

"I can't make them do it." Asher scratched his head. "Have you ever tried to make those three do anything?"

"Every day, and I can assure you that it is possible." For goodness' sake, how did the man enforce the law if he couldn't handle three young boys? "My toes are frozen through, Sheriff. Thank you for the warning concerning the pastor. Tell your nephews I will see them at school tomorrow and that they had better have a portion of the script written or they will be doing extra ciphering as a discipline."

She stormed into the house, slammed the door and leaned against the painted wood, gently banging her head. What in the world had she done to deserve such a thorn in her side as the impossible Thomas boys?

As reluctant as she was to do so, Charlotte headed for her battered table, prepared to write her college instructor a letter, asking for advice. Anyone with the notion to look hard enough could tell Charlotte was in over her head.

Not only with the Thomas boys, but also the silly feud that threatened to tear her school apart. Not to mention how rattled the sheriff left her after every encounter.

That woman and her orders. Of course, Asher had almost lost his resolve not to sing when tears sprang to her eyes, but that went away right quick when she started barking at him. That woman was as soft and cuddly as a kitten one minute and as prickly as a porcupine the next.

Asher swung into the saddle. He'd mention to the boys the importance of keeping their word and do everything he could to make sure they went along with what they'd promised. He'd only wanted to warn her that school on Monday might be a little difficult.

Instead, he heard how she was going to another man's house for supper. A man who, besides the feud, had a lot more to offer a woman than Asher did. What woman wanted to marry a lawman in a small mountain town? Or wed a man who disappeared at every opportunity to find out information about his missing brother? No. Asher had resigned himself long ago to the fact that marriage was far in his future.

His head told him he'd made the right choice, but when he laid eyes on Charlotte, he was tempted to change his mind. Life with such a fiery woman would not be boring. The woman could cook, sew, nurse, tend the young'uns. Yep, whatever man got hitched up with her would be one lucky fella. He almost wished it could be him.

Chapter 8

Charlotte glanced around the home of Hank Jones. Faded newsprint covered walls in a vain attempt to keep out the cold. Greased paper covered unshuttered windows. Faded, yellow gingham fabric hung on each side of the windows. A pot-bellied stove sat in one corner of the shack, and all eight family members, plus Charlotte, crowded around it in an attempt to keep warm.

Maybe she should have put off visiting the homes of her students until spring. But she needed to learn practical ways to help the students in her care.

And learning she was, indeed, in this string of visits. Hopefully, it would be more pleasant than her visit with the pastor, who still seemed to believe Charlotte welcomed his attentions. This mountain home was the third she'd visited that week. The occupants sorely needed lessons in home cleanliness and repair. Charlotte chewed on the inside of her cheek. How could she offer help without harming the family's pride? Why hadn't someone taught them simple hygienic procedures? Sure, she'd noticed the children's patched clothing each day at school, and the threadbare jackets, but their faces were always freshly scrubbed and their hair slicked into place. Why didn't the homes reflect the same pride?

The middle child, Lila Rose, would make a perfect angel for the play, if only Charlotte could get her to speak. Eight years old and sharp as a tack, at least on paper, and she had yet to speak a single word at school. Her siblings said she chattered like a magpie at home.

"Supper's done." Mrs. Jones wiped her hands across a stained apron and stood beside a table set with stone crockery. "Rabbit stew, freshly killed this morning by my boy, Frank."

Charlotte always thought wild rabbit tasted a bit gamey, but plastered a smile on her face. These people had so little, yet were happy to share their dinner with her. She stared into the bowl in front of the seat they ushered her toward at the far end of a wooden bench, clearly meant for guests. Inside the bowl lay pearl onions and strips of meat in a watery broth. A pan of corn pone sat in the center of the table. "It looks delicious."

"My wife is a right fine cook." Mr. Jones reached for the pan of bread. "Eat up, Teacher, there's plenty."

"Thank you." Charlotte lifted her spoon. Dried bits of food clung to the pewter. On the pretense of dropping the utensil, Charlotte wiped it on her skirt.

"Let me fetch you another," Mrs. Jones offered.

"Oh, no, thank you. I've wiped it clean. A little dirt never hurt anyone." Charlotte cringed at her white lie then noted the deepening dusk outside. She wanted to be home before dark and still needed to bring up the subject of the Christmas play.

"Is there something on your mind, Teacher?" Mr. Jones broke his corn pone into pieces and dropped it in his bowl of stew.

"Actually, there is." Charlotte set her spoon beside her bowl. "I dearly want Frank to play the part of Joseph in the play. Your other children would be shepherds and angels, except for Lila Rose. I'm hoping she could be the angel who brings the good tidings to the shepherds."

He narrowed his eyes. "You got that Sweeney gal playing Mary, don'tcha?"

She took a deep breath. "Yes, sir."

"Do they have to talk to each other? Look at each other? Anything like that?"

"Uh." Charlotte opened her mouth, closed it, then opened it again, unsure whether the man was serious about his question. "There will be a few speaking parts, certainly, but these will be derived from the Bible, spoken more to the audience than the cast members."

Mr. Jones glanced around the table at the faces of his children. "I reckon it's all right, as long as they don't mingle too much or start making friends with Sweeneys."

"God bless you, Mr. Jones." Charlotte's grin hurt her cheeks it was so wide. Mr. Jones had a more charitable heart than the town's pastor.

Her dinner with him had been anything but pleasant. Not only had she provided the meal, but assisted Lucy in cleaning up while Pastor Sweeney propped his feet on a stool and smoked a smelly pipe, then laid out his conditions for the play. The only way he'd agree for Lucy to attend rehearsals was if he were also present. Then, and only then, he would determine whether his daughter would go through with the performance. The arrogance! Never before had Charlotte met a man of God who seemed more lip service than heart.

"God has already blessed me beyond measure." Mr. Jones patted his wife's hand then rubbed her very swollen stomach.

The man's obvious love for his wife overshadowed the dismal surroundings of the cabin. As much as Charlotte wanted to help them understand the need for a clean, sanitary home, she didn't want to come across as judgmental. Especially not after seeing how the family related to each other. Pastor Sweeney's home had been spotless, yet the man ruled over his daughter with barked orders and harsh words. Poverty did not mean a life of unhappiness. She decided to keep quiet.

Charlotte finished her stew and offered her thanks, her heart warmed by the love and acceptance of the Jones family. If only she could bottle their kindness and shake it over the rest of Plumville. "I look forward to seeing all of you at school tomorrow."

"They'll be there." Mr. Jones walked her to the door, then closed it behind her.

Charlotte's smile faded. Where was Blue? She'd left him tied to the splintered porch railing. Oh, that animal. She wrapped her arms around her in an attempt to ward off the cold and began her long trudge home.

Muddy hoofprints showed on top of the crusty ground, along with three sizes of bootprints. Charlotte clenched her jaw. Those Thomas boys had to stop pestering her or she'd take a switch to them herself.

Instead of heading home, she changed directions. Her anger kept her warm enough as she stomped to the Thomas cabin. Tied by the road, head down and looking as forlorn as Charlotte felt, was Blue. Poor thing must be half-frozen.

Charlotte pounded on the cabin door. "Open up this instant."

The door opened an inch and one blue eye peered out. "Why, it's Miss Nelson. Won't you come in?"

She shoved her way past Matthew and made a beeline to the fireplace. "Where is your uncle? I demand to know why you stole my mule and left me to freeze as I walked home."

"I'm interested in hearing the answer to that as well, boys." Asher entered through a back door, scrubbing his head with a towel.

He snapped the towel over the back of a chair and glared at Matthew, then at the loft where the other two stared down. "All of you at the table. Now." Hadn't they already gone through the dangers of leaving the teacher outside in the cold? "Explain yourselves."

Charlotte turned her back to the fire. "I'd just finished an enjoyable meal at Frank Jones's place when I step outside to find my mule gone. I followed the tracks here and—"

"You followed the tracks?" He didn't think she knew how, especially after getting lost in the woods.

She stiffened. "I paid attention the last time, Sheriff. Contrary to your obvious opinion, I can be taught."

"That wasn't what I was thinking at all. I was only surprised that—"

"Surprised that a city girl could learn to follow tracks? Mr. Thomas, the tracks the boys left were easy enough for a child to follow."

"Were they now?" He transferred his attention back to the boys. They'd wanted her to follow. There was no other explanation. "Explain, Matthew. As the oldest, I hold you personally responsible."

The boy's eyes cut to his teacher's. "She's been going to everybody else's house for dinner and ain't been by here in a long time." His face reddened. "How y'all supposed to get hitched if you ain't together?"

"Oh, my." Charlotte stepped back, then jumped forward as the hem of her skirt caught fire.

Asher lunged forward and stomped it out, leaving a scorched hole the size of a flapjack.

When he was sure the fire was out, he stepped back. "Sorry."

"Thank you. It was my fault." She held her dress out to examine the hole.

He turned to the boys. "We've talked about this before. Miss Nelson and I are not getting hitched." What was he going to do with those three? "I want all of you to write out the Ten Commandments ten times."

"But it's bedtime," Mark wailed.

"You should have thought of that before endangering Miss Nelson's life again." Asher would not be swayed by freckles and tears. Not this time. "Miss Nelson, I will escort you home. Boys, I expect you to still be sitting at this table when I return." He grabbed his coat and hat, then yanked open the front door.

A wide-eyed Charlotte scooted past him. He hoped she was happy witnessing his scolding of the boys. What he did in the privacy of his own home should stay there. He didn't cotton to hanging dirty laundry on the line. Now maybe the teacher would get off his back about being too easy on the rascals.

After checking the cinch on Blue, Asher helped Charlotte mount, trying to ignore the way her small waist felt in his hands, or the soft scent of rose toilet water. He turned to ready his horse. He paused, resting his forehead on the saddle. "I apologize for the boys. They mean well." He swung into his seat.

"They only want a mother." Her soft words drifted across the crisp air.

"I don't even know if they still have a pa." And with the boys' behavior not improving, Asher would have to lay aside the desire to locate his brother and focus instead on the important responsibility laid at his doorstep.

"Your visits with the townsfolk going okay?" he asked as they rode toward her place.

"Yes, very much so." She sighed. "Although I do worry about Lucy. But the love of Hank Jones for his family is heartwarming. And there is one family, the Colsons, that I worry about. Not to mention the deplorable poverty rampant in this hollow."

"You can't help the poverty. These are a proud people that make do for themselves, as they have for centuries. What concerns you about the Colsons?"

"The oldest boy, Georgie, was out chopping wood without a shirt on. He had bruises, much like fingermarks, on his upper arm. He also had a strap mark on his back. It's obvious someone beat him. And does the boy not own any warm clothing? He wears a shirt to school, but he didn't have a coat on today. I should have noticed earlier."

"How did Ben Colson treat you?" Asher wished he had known she was going over there. The man wasn't known for his kind treatment of women. Or anyone, for that matter. If he was abusing his son, Asher would need to pay a call on him.

"He was fine. Didn't let me into the house nor offer me a drink. I gather there's no woman in the picture?"

"Don't ever go into Ben Colson's home," Asher said

gravely. "In fact, don't go anywhere near him without someone with you. I mean it, Charlie, uh, Charlotte. The man is dangerous."

"All right. I am amazed at the response to the play, though. Everyone seems to embrace the idea—as long as I can keep the Joneses from talking to the Sweeneys. It's the most ridiculous thing I've ever heard. I'm thinking of making Georgie a robe that can double as a coat so he has something warm to wear. Maybe I can write to my mother's church and…"

"Did you hear me? Stay away from Ben Colson."

"I heard you." She tilted her chin and glared. "But I will not stand aside from a child in need without helping. I've decided not to force lessons on cleanliness and hygiene on the people of Plumville, but I can help a child."

"Well, thank the Lord for small favors."

"Don't be sarcastic. It's unbecoming."

The woman was like a burr under his saddle. "These people won't accept your charity."

"It won't be charity. They'll just get to keep their costumes. I have it all figured out." She grinned, her teeth flashing white in the moonlight, sending prickles up his spine. "Don't worry."

Those words alone make his skin crawl. Not worry? All he did around the teacher was worry. "Miss Nelson. Charlotte. I don't even know what to call you." He wanted to call her Charlie just to see sparks fly from her eyes. "You need to take my words seriously. Most of the time, these are the finest people you'll ever meet, but you're an outsider with highfalutin ideas. You want them to mingle in a Christmas play. You're trying to get them to get along after years of fighting. All this adds up to is a match in a barrel of gunpowder."

"Oh, pooh. Surely you exaggerate. How can they not be pleased that I am working with, I dare say helping, their children?" She shrugged. "It's unfathomable. And how can the local pastor be part of the feud?"

"I don't know how he does it," Asher admitted. "But the man has shown that he can set aside his mantle of prejudice when one of his flock needs him, Jones or Sweeney. It's a real mystery."

Charlotte clutched her mother's letter to her chest and did a very unladylike jig around the cabin. Even the cold wood floor under her slippers couldn't detract from her good mood. A private school in Savannah had an opening the next fall and was seriously considering Charlotte for the position. Sending out applications to schools around the country had definitely been worth the time. Her dreams were close to coming true.

Not to mention the arrival of a crate full of school supplies and secondhand clothing lying at her feet. The ladies of her mother's church had gone above and beyond what Charlotte asked of them. Each child in the school would receive a brand-new slate and box of chalk, along with several articles of clothing that somehow Charlotte needed to make into costumes in order to get around the hill people's dislike of charity.

There were also shoes and yards of fabric. How could she possibly get the items into the right hands? She would need to ask Asher. He would know how she could do so without offending anyone.

A colorful quilt of red and blue now lay across the back of Charlotte's rocking chair. It was meant for Georgie Colson, who would receive a coat of many colors, just like Joseph in the Bible. If she transformed the quilt into a shepherd's robe of some kind, his father couldn't be upset in the slightest, and the boy would be warm through a frigid mountain winter.

She plopped in the chair and read her mother's letter again. Seeing how much her parents missed her warmed her heart. But in a few months, they could again be in the same city if Charlotte began teaching at the fancy private school. She sat back and propped her feet on a small crate she used as an ottoman and stared into the fire.

The excitement coursing through her waned. If she received and accepted the job in Savannah, she'd have to leave Plumville and the students. She'd have to leave Asher and his three rowdy nephews. A smile tugged at her lips. She loved those boys, rascals that they were, and if she were honest with herself, she had growing feelings for their uncle, as well.

She couldn't stay, though. Not when she was so close to fulfilling her dreams. But she was beginning to feel doubts about those dreams. She fiddled with the lace at her throat. What if teaching in a big school wasn't part of God's will for her? The Bible said He gave His children the desires of their heart, but what if Charlotte didn't know what her heart really wanted?

Could it be possible that God intended her to stay in a small Ozark mountain town full of strife and prejudice? Surely not. But then again…there was the handsome sheriff. Asher's face swam before her. Her heart thumped harder. She needed to spend some serious time in prayer before accepting or declining the private school's offer. If she even received one.

A glance at the porcelain clock on the mantel sent her scurrying to get dressed. How pleased the children would be when she presented them with their new supplies. Almost as tickled as she'd been to discover the

crate on the doorstep when she'd awoken. Bless who-
ever had kindly delivered it to her.

Asher huddled before the fireplace, a mug of hot coffee warming his hands. He smiled, guessing at Charlotte's reaction to the crate beside her door. Her pretty
face would light up with her smile, and those winter-
blue eyes would sparkle with light. Maybe he should've
stuck around to see her expression, but that early in the
morning would most likely have her in her nightclothes.
His face heated, remembering that time he'd had to
rescue her from a coon stuck in the school flue. No, it
wouldn't do to be in that particular circumstance again.

"Boys! Hurry up or you'll be late for school. Doesn't
play practice start today?" Asher tilted his head and
glanced at the loft where one by one the boys' frowning faces appeared.

"We ain't staying for that!" Matthew yelled before
withdrawing.

"Yes, you are." Asher set his mug on the stone hearth
and stood. "You've got five minutes to get down here
and eat."

"If you ain't going to sing, we ain't going to act or
write that stupid play."

Mark and Luke looked from Asher to Matthew, their
faces pale, and scuttered backward.

"You'll do the play if I have to be there watching
every afternoon." Asher planted his fists on his hips.
His neck heated. "If you give Miss Nelson any trouble,
I'll tan your hides."

"You ain't never hit us and won't start now!"

Asher sighed. The boy was right. He'd never laid
a hand on them in anger. There wasn't any hope for
it. He'd have to sing in front of the whole hollow. His

stomach churned just thinking about it. "Fine. You win. I'll sing. But don't you breathe one word of it to your teacher. I don't want her thinking she's won this battle so quickly."

Matthew peered back from the loft. "Really? You ain't just saying that so you can back out later?"

"No, I promise." Asher shook his head. Maybe an emergency would pull him away by then.

"Okay, but we're not writing the play. Teacher keeps bugging us to, but I think she's gonna do it. Besides, my spelling is awful." He withdrew again and soon all three boys clambered down the ladder.

Miss Nelson would have to take what she could get. Asher plopped oatmeal into four bowls and set them on the table. He'd send a note with the boys informing her of their decision not to write the script, and prayed she wouldn't be too disappointed in his failure to make them do it. If the boys were forced, the play would be a travesty, and that would be worse than her having to write it herself.

After wolfing down his food, he scribbled a quick note, shoved it in Luke's pocket without the other two seeing, and whispered strict orders for no one to see the note except for the teacher. Luke nodded solemnly. If the two older boys found out Asher had written a note, they'd most likely rip it to shreds and toss it on the side of the path. As it was, Asher would have to make a point of being at the school when it let out for the day, just to make sure the first day's rehearsal went without shenanigans.

"Never mind." He fished the note back out of Luke's pocket. "I'm riding with y'all to school today. I'll deliver it myself."

The ride to school was silent except for the rustling

of leafless tree branches and the crunch of ice under the horses' hooves. No doubt the boys wanted to know what Asher's note said. They could wallow in their curiosity. He chuckled, envisioning their faces when he showed up for rehearsal.

The school day finally ended. The students' excitement over something as simple as new school supplies had carried into the afternoon, making simple lessons a chore to teach. Charlotte smoothed her hair back into a bun and faced the room of squirming children. Asher's note about the boys' refusal to write the play crackled in her pocket. Disappointment had threatened to shadow the day, but she'd managed to shove it aside and focus on the faces of every student behind a battered desk.

She cleared her throat to get everyone's attention. Once all eyes were focused on her, she proceeded. "Today is the first day of our work on our play. I will assign roles, and I hope by next Monday to have a script to hand out." She narrowed her eyes at the Thomas boys. "I'll have to spend my evenings writing it, but all is well." She rubbed her hands together. "Is there anyone here who will not be participating?"

No hands rose, but furtive glances from several of the Jones students to the Sweeneys increased Charlotte's fear. "I really need to know—"

"They'll all be there." Asher banged through the door, stomping the mud from his boots. "I'll make sure the parents see the good that will come of having the play."

"Nobody makes up my mind." Pastor Sweeney entered behind him and took up guard at the back of the room, his arms crossed. "I'm holding out on letting Lucy commit."

"But, Pastor, she's to play the part of Mary." Charlotte returned his glare. "She's perfect."

He grinned. "Perhaps you could entertain us with your wonderful cooking again this Sunday? We could further discuss your plans for my daughter."

Charlotte's eyes widened. Had the man really asked her to bring food again? She glanced at Asher. A muscle twitched in his jaw as he cut a sideways glance at the other man. The students sat still as statues in their seats, watching the drama unfold.

"Sir, I'm afraid I can't spend more time at one student's home than the others." She shook her head, forcing a smile to her face. "It wouldn't be—"

"That's right, Sweeney." Asher nodded. "She's coming to my place this Sunday."

Charlotte blinked, her smile fading. The Thomas boys grinned like loons. Oh, my. She could see what was happening here, and she wanted no part in it. If the two men wanted to play top rooster they could do it outside. Not to mention the fact she had the niggling feeling they were fighting over her.

"Gentlemen, I must ask you to take your conversation outside." She tilted her chin. "The children and I have work to do."

"Well, whose house are you visiting this Sunday?" Although the question was aimed at her, the pastor's gaze never left Asher's face.

"That is my business." She marched between the desks and held open the door. "Gentlemen."

"I'll be waiting right outside for my Lucy." The pastor's grin faded. "If I hear any funny stuff—" his finger wagged between Frank and Lucy "—I'll be back in here faster than a bee-stung mule."

"I'll keep a close eye on them, I promise." Charlotte nodded toward the door. "You, too, Sheriff."

"But, I, uh, wanted to talk to you." He scratched his head.

"About?"

"Uh...did you get the crate all right?"

"I did. Were you the one who delivered it to me? I'm obliged. There was also a letter from my mother, which pleased me very much. Thank you." She opened the door farther.

"Good news, I hope." He twisted his hat.

"Very. A school position I've been considering will be opening soon."

His face paled, and a vein in his temple throbbed. Slapping his hat on his head, he whirled and stormed outside, leaving Charlotte feeling as if she'd delivered bad news.

Chapter 9

Charlotte rubbed her hand over the "coat of many colors" designed for Georgie Colson. She'd given him the part of head shepherd, her heart warmed by the pleasure radiating from his face when she'd told him his role. How would he act when she handed him the robe?

She folded the costume, gathered her bag full of scripts and headed outside, closing the door to her cabin behind her. She'd already put together the other costumes and wanted to show each child theirs at the day's rehearsal. Thanksgiving was next week, so there'd be few rehearsals until after the holiday.

Hunching in her coat against the winter chill, she trudged toward the schoolhouse, thankful the townspeople had thought to build her cabin and the school close together. Savannah never got the type of cold that bit at one's fingers and burrowed to the bone. Since she'd wasted precious minutes putting the final touches on

Georgie's costume, the school wouldn't be warm when the students arrived. How could she have let the time get away from her?

Once inside the schoolhouse, she stomped her feet, bringing feeling back to her toes, and placed wood in the stove. Why hadn't she prepared the stove the night before? Because she needed to finish the script and play schedule, that's why. Oh, if only the townspeople were more accommodating. Then she could have asked Lucy to write the script since the Thomas boys had refused. The girl was certainly bright enough.

Finally, a small flame flickered to life among the pieces of kindling, and Charlotte practically hugged the stove. If she weren't careful, she'd burn herself. She still mourned her favorite skirt, and tried to figure out a way to salvage it. Maybe a strategically placed swatch of lace? She shivered. Why was she worried about an article of clothing when the room was freezing?

She stuck her hands in her armpits and glanced around, deciding what needed to be done first. Maybe the students could gather around the stove while doing their arithmetic exercises. By then, the room would have warmed enough to start the other lessons.

The students trickled in, their breath forming plumes in front of their faces. Charlotte apologized to each one as they gathered around the stove and promised to never let duties distract her to the point of a cold school again.

"That's okay, Teacher," Molly, the youngest Colson child, said. She shivered under a threadbare blanket. "We hardly have heat at home. Georgie and me are used to being cold."

Charlotte's heart tightened. She'd assigned the adorable dark-haired girl the role of one of the angels in the heavenly choir, but the white costume she'd wear wasn't nearly as warm as Georgie's robe would be. How could she get these people to accept warm clothing, even secondhand? The children shouldn't have to suffer because of the parents' pride.

The skirt! Charlotte would recycle her warm skirt into a coat for the child, and she would let Molly's father know it was useless as it was to her the way it was because of the hole. She grinned and clapped her hands. The gesture sent prickles through her cold fingers. "Gather your slates, students. We'll do our arithmetic around the stove this morning."

The Thomas boys thundered into the room and skidded to a halt so sudden that their uncle bumped into them. "It's freezing in here." Asher glanced around the room. "Would you like me to come early each morning and start the fire for you?"

Charlotte sighed. "No, thank you. This is only a one-time lapse. I assure you it won't happen again. But if you have a moment, Mr. Thomas, I'd like a word."

"Sure, but make it fast." He pulled his coat tighter around him and eyed the stove. "It's bitter cold, and I've a trip to take up the mountain."

"We'll step into the corner." Charlotte led the way behind her desk and lowered her voice. "I'm sure you know how impoverished the Colson children are. How unkindly will their father take to the notion of me recycling an article of clothing that is no longer of use to me into a coat for Molly?"

He shrugged. "You never can tell with that man." He narrowed his eyes. "But remember…you promised not to go over there alone again."

"I won't. I'll give her the coat at school in a few days, or better yet, at church on Sunday. Do the Colsons attend? I don't recall seeing them at the last service."

"No, they don't. That mean skunk would never step foot in a church." Asher shuddered. "I can take the coat over and try to talk sense into the man."

"Bless you." Charlotte clapped her hands. "I'll let you know when it's ready."

Asher nodded. "Is there rehearsal after school today?"

"Yes. I'll hand out the scripts today, and we won't rehearse again until after Thanksgiving."

"Will the pastor be here?"

Charlotte stared into Asher's hazel eyes. The worry in them almost caused her to lie. As much as she enjoyed the handsome sheriff's attention, and the way her wayward heart skipped when he strolled anywhere near, she didn't want to attract any man's attention. Not when her dreams were so close to fruition. She sighed. "Yes."

"Then I'll see you after school." He gave a curt nod and stormed out the door.

Why was Sweeney all of a sudden hanging around the school? It wasn't because he was trying to decide whether or not to let Lucy play Mary. Of course the man would let her play the part. After all, any chance to get his daughter into the main role would boost his pride. But Asher suspected him of an ulterior motive. One that chilled his heart. Sweeney was after a new wife—and had his sights on Charlotte.

Asher slapped his hat against his thigh. Why should he care? He'd told himself for years that a wife wasn't in his foreseeable future. But Charlotte Nelson was the prettiest thing he'd ever seen. If any woman could change his mind about marriage, it would be her. So if the preacher was going to show up at every rehearsal, then Asher would, too.

Maybe, while doing so, he could change Charlotte's mind about leaving Plumville and teaching at that fancy school in Georgia. He swung into his saddle and headed north. He'd heard rumors that his brother might be making moonshine on a far ridge. If Asher hurried, he'd have time to check out the information and still make it in time for rehearsal.

The faces of the Colson children filtered through his mind. Ben Colson had never recovered from the death of his wife—a death at the man's own hands, nonetheless. A movement in the brush while she hunted for mushrooms. The pull of the hunter's trigger. Some said Colson had killed her on purpose because she liked the other fellas too much, but Asher had never been able to prove it anything but an accident. Either way, the man mourned by spending his days immersed in a bottle and forgetting about his children.

But Asher had never given up hope that Ben would wake up. What the man needed was a good woman to turn him around.

Asher laughed, the sound ringing across the ridge, no doubt alerting anyone within hearing distance. Here he was saying how a woman could help a man and yet, he didn't feel he needed one in his own life. Something changed when he set eyes on a spirited, raven-haired woman with blue-gray eyes.

"Here are the songs and speaking parts." Charlotte handed each child what they would need to memorize and tried to ignore the stares of Pastor Sweeney. He leaned against the far wall, his gaze never leaving her. "When we return after Thanksgiving, we'll have our first full rehearsal. Please take time during the holiday break to learn your lines and the words to each song.

Also, any poems and readings not yet turned in will be due at that time." She scanned the room. "We want this to be the best pageant Plumville has ever seen."

"It's the only pageant," Matthew stated. "None of the other teachers wanted the bother, I guess."

"Then we want it extra special, don't we?" She motioned for Georgie to approach her desk. When he did, eyes wide, she smiled. "Relax. You aren't in trouble. I have your costume for the play and thought you might want it early." Charlotte dug the robe from the crate at her feet and handed it to him.

His eyes lit up like the candles on a Christmas tree. "That's the nicest thing I've ever seen, Miss Nelson. I'm afraid to wear it. What if I get it dirty?"

"It'll wash." She moved to his side and helped him put it on. "It fits perfectly." Best of all, the quilted robe would protect him from the cold.

"It's big enough to drape over me and Molly on our way home."

Charlotte ruffled the boy's hair. "Bless you for thinking of your sister. You're a wonderful big brother."

He puffed out his chest. "I promised Ma I would look after Molly. I aim to keep that promise."

"You're doing a—"

The door to the school banged open, and Mr. Colson stomped in. "What's taking this practice time so long?" He glowered at Georgie. "Take that off and get in the wagon."

"Students, you're dismissed." Charlotte gave Georgie's shoulder a squeeze and approached his father. "I apologize for rehearsal running later than usual. I completed your son's costume and wanted him to try it on. It's a perfect fit." She gave the man a shaky smile.

"Since the weather has turned frightful, I thought he could use it as a coat until the play."

Mr. Colson stormed to the front of the room and grabbed his son's arm. "I said to take it off. We don't need this city woman's charity."

Georgie shrugged out of the robe, tears shimmering in his eyes.

Flames lit in Charlotte. "Mr. Colson! There is no need for you to manhandle the child. He's done nothing wrong."

He pointed a finger in her face. "You stay out of my business or you'll be sorry. These are my young'uns and I take good care of them."

"It's freezing outside." She tilted her chin and crossed her arms. "I also have an old skirt that has a burn mark in it that I'm fashioning into a coat for Molly. All of the students will be able to keep their costumes. It's not charity, Mr. Colson."

"That ain't the way I see it." He yanked Georgie forward.

"Going somewhere in a hurry, Ben?" Asher shouldered through the door. "My apologies, Miss Nelson, my work took longer than expected."

"Move out of my way, Sheriff." Ben tried to shove past.

"Aren't you forgetting something?" Asher grinned, white teeth flashing.

"Like what?"

"The boy's robe. It's starting to snow."

"We have no need for that woman's castoffs." Ben Colson's face darkened.

"Even you are wearing a coat, Ben." Asher rubbed the arms of the patched wool coat. "Don't your children deserve the same?"

"Get the robe, Georgie." Ben glared at Charlotte. "This ain't over, Miss Nelson. Not by a long shot. Molly, quit hiding behind her skirt and get in the wagon."

"Expect a visit from me if that robe disappears, gets ruined, or your children sport bruises." Asher tipped his hat. "Happy Thanksgiving."

The man cursed and marched outside.

Charlotte sagged into her chair. "That man is frightening. He all but threatened me."

"He did threaten you, Charlotte." Asher planted his palms flat on her desk. "Take great care when you're out and about."

"I'd be happy to offer my services of protection," Pastor Sweeney added, approaching the desk.

Charlotte almost mentioned how little he had helped while the man threatened her just moments before. Instead, she focused on the dimple in Asher's chin and how easily he'd managed to get Ben Colson to accept the robe. With threats, but at least the young boy would be warm. She blinked away tears. "Thank you, Asher."

Charlotte read the note tacked on her door inviting her to Thanksgiving dinner at the Sweeney residence in two days. She wrinkled her nose. No doubt the dear pastor would want her to bring all the fixings, too. No, she'd rather stay home than squirm under his stare or answer questions about why she wasn't married, each word part of a game to ensnare her in the man's clutches.

Although Duke Sweeney had yet to offer her marriage, his intentions were as clear as mountain creek water. If he should ask, and Charlotte refused, what would that do to her already tenuous acceptance into life among the people of Plumville? How would they accept an outsider's rejection of their pastor, strange as it was? It still baffled her how a man of God could be involved in a feud six out of seven days, yet tend to his flock on the seventh, and everyone seemed fine with the arrangement. Back home, the pastor had a smile for everyone, every day of the week.

The growing feelings she had for Asher didn't help. If she spent Thanksgiving anywhere other than alone, or with her parents in Savannah, she wanted it to be at the Thomas cabin. Unfortunately, no invitation had come her way from that quarter. She'd heard tales that the Widow Slater had her eye on the sheriff. Maybe Asher and the boys would spend the holiday with her. The woman was comely enough, with her flaxen hair and hazel eyes. She was one of the hill people and would no doubt suit Asher well.

The thought stabbed Charlotte. What a fool she was. With no intentions of settling down, she shouldn't allow her wayward heart to have such feelings for a man she could never have. Not with her plans for the future.

She ripped the note from the door and stepped back into her cabin. Wise or not, she didn't want to be alone on Thanksgiving, and there was no one in Plumville she'd rather spend the day with than Asher.

Maybe she'd feel better by baking her mother's famous pecan pie. She could take it by the Thomas place and maybe finagle an invitation. She giggled. Her mother would be ashamed of the thought. Ladies did not invite themselves anywhere. But what did Charlotte have to lose?

Charlotte tossed the note in the fireplace, grabbed her warmest cloak and headed out to saddle Blue. The mule balked at being led into the cold wind, only venturing out when Charlotte enticed him with a carrot.

"Come on, boy. I know it's cold, but I've a pie to bake

and none of the ingredients on hand." She led him to the mounting stump and climbed into the saddle. Times like these, when she had to make the trip to the mercantile and back, she sorely missed her papa's riding horses. Blue's rough trot always left her sore.

By the time she reached the mercantile, her body felt bruised despite her frozen limbs. She longed for spring with its gentle breezes and the warmth of summer with its humidity and brilliant blue sky. Who was she kidding? She wouldn't be in the mountains by summer. Instead, she'd be back in Savannah, mopping the perspiration off her face with a towel and behaving as a well-mannered woman should.

After tying Blue to the hitching post, Charlotte pushed open the mercantile door. A bell tinkled overhead. "Happy Thanksgiving, Mrs. Mabry." Charlotte unwound her scarf and headed for the stove where two gentlemen sat—the same two who had sat there on her first day. Maybe they were permanent fixtures in the store. "Good morning, gentlemen."

"Teacher." Hank gave a nod in greeting. "Buying more things for that play of yours?"

"No, sir. Not this time." Charlotte grinned. "I'm purchasing the ingredients for a pie, although I do pray you'll join us for the pageant. You won't be disappointed." She winked. "You can sit on the Joneses' side of the building."

"Saucy woman." Hank's eyes twinkled. "Like I'd sit anywhere else."

Charlotte laughed and held her hands over the stove's heat. "I wish you families would let go of this silly feud. It's almost 1882. Feuding is of ancient times."

"You tell Sweeney to let go, and I'll let go. It's his family that won't let the grudge drop." Hank scowled.

"The missus is hankering for you to come visit again. We'll talk at church after Thanksgiving."

"I'll look forward to the invitation." Charlotte moved to the counter where Mrs. Mabry waited. "I'm baking a pecan pie. Please, tell me you have all the ingredients on this recipe." She pulled a slip of paper from her pocket and handed it to the storekeeper.

Mrs. Mabry scanned the list. "I sure do. Heat yourself some more and I'll be right with you."

Instead of heading back to the stove, Charlotte browsed the shelves, her gaze landing on a bolt of navy blue velvet. She could make a lovely Christmas dress. It had been so long since she'd had a new dress. There was even a yard of lovely lace in the crate her mother sent, perfect for adorning a collar and cuffs. Considering how often she used to buy a new frock or two, she was way overdue for a new gown. She mentally calculated her funds then hefted the heavy bolt and plopped it on the counter.

"I'd also like six yards of this." She could imagine how Asher's eyes would light up when he saw her wearing the beautiful shade of blue.

By the time Charlotte had arrived back home and baked her pie, the day's shadows had lengthened. If she didn't want to be caught outside after dark, she needed to hurry to Asher's. The walk would take more than half an hour. Riding Blue with a pie in her hands was out of the question, unless she wanted the dessert to arrive in pieces.

She wrapped her cloak around her and stepped outside. The brisk air and sharp wind took her breath away. Some would call her a fool for venturing out in such cold, but unless Charlotte wanted to spend Thanks-

giving alone she'd have to take the chance that her pie
would win her an invitation.

Teeth chattering, and reconsidering the wisdom
of her forward actions, Charlotte raised her hand and
rapped on the door of Asher's home. As usual, she'd
rushed ahead with her plans instead of praying and
waiting for an answer from God.

The loud voices of the boys rose on the other side
of the wood. She couldn't do this. No proper woman
coerced a man into an invitation. She turned to leave.

The door opened. "Charlotte?" Asher stepped outside, stopping her.

Charlotte closed her eyes and took a deep breath.
Then, opening her eyes and squaring her shoulders, she
turned and thrust the pie toward him. "I've brought you
a pie. Happy Thanksgiving."

"Thank you." Asher took the pie before it fell from
Charlotte's trembling hands. "Come in." He stepped
aside and allowed her to enter first. His mind whirled
at the unexpected visit. Had the boys been up to more
mischief? Had Colson paid her a visit? He set the pie on
the table and helped Charlotte out of her wrap.

"You must be half-frozen. Here. Sit." He led her to
his favorite chair and then coaxed the flames in the fire
to burn hotter. "Is something wrong?"

She shook her head. "No. I…uh…just wanted to
bring you a pie." She cringed.

Asher scratched his head and glanced at the loft from
which the three boys stared down, questions on their
faces. "Any special reason?"

"All your help?" Her mouth twitched.

"Are you asking me?" He sat in the hard rocking
chair across from her.

She giggled then clamped a hand over her mouth, her eyes brimming. "Forgive me." She giggled again and wiped her eyes. "You'll think me foolish."

"I doubt that." Although her strange behavior was starting to worry him. "Did the boys do something?"

"We didn't do anything!" Matthew scowled. "Not even cook up a reason for her to come."

Charlotte's shoulders shook with silent laughter. "No, I just wanted to bring you a pie."

"All right." Asher waved a hand, signaling for the boys to duck out of sight. "Would you like some coffee to go with the pie? We could enjoy a piece right now." The thought pleased him. She'd come on her own accord with no other obvious reason than that she wanted his company. He told himself not to read anything more into the situation than that, but his heart leaped, anyway.

"I would love a cup." Charlotte stood and moved to the table. "If you'll hand me plates, I'll slice the pie."

Coffee poured and slices of pie in front of them, Asher held his fork suspended and stared across the table at Charlotte. He still thought it odd that she would show up with dusk beginning to fall and with no other pretense than to offer a pie. But what did he know? He was certainly no expert on women. Maybe they did this type of thing all the time. The Widow Slater never seemed to have second thoughts about bringing food by, but then again she had her sight set on...he dropped his fork. Had Charlotte set her cap for him?

He studied her raven hair, falling loose from its bun, shimmering like the night sky after a summer rain. Then she lifted those wondrous eyes his way, and he knew for a fact he needed to tell the widow not to send any more food for him and the boys. If Charlotte found out, and she did have intentions toward Asher, they'd stop accepting gifts from the widow or Charlotte would want nothing more to do with him. He didn't want that to happen.

He lifted his fork and took a bite of sweet pecan pie. If he were like the pastor and judging a wife's worth by her cooking, Charlotte would win hands down over anyone in the hollow.

"Are you spending Thanksgiving with the Widow Slater?" Charlotte dabbed her mouth with a napkin, fixing those amazing eyes on him.

Asher choked and grabbed for his coffee. Had she read his mind? "Didn't plan on it, why?" He forced his answer once he could breathe.

"Seems I've heard from a few folks that you two might have an agreement." Charlotte shrugged.

"No, I can't say that we do." His throat still wanted to seize. What was Charlotte trying to say? He sipped the too-hot coffee in a poor attempt at soothing his tortured throat.

"I have a confession." She placed her fork carefully beside her plate. "I have ulterior motives for bringing you this pie." She ducked her head. "I don't wish to spend Thanksgiving alone and came hoping for an invitation." She raised a hand when he opened his mouth to speak. "Please forgive me for my brashness, but this is my first holiday away from home and…my cabin is too small, but I thought, maybe, if I brought all the fixings, you could provide the turkey and we could—"

Asher placed his hand over hers. "Miss Nelson, would you kindly accept my invitation to Thanksgiving? I'd be proud to bag the turkey if you'd cook it."

Suddenly, Thanksgiving promised to be the best day of the year so far.

Chapter 10

Charlotte basted the turkey, a fine fifteen-pounder Asher had shot the day before, then turned to the kitchen table where Luke waited to play a game of checkers with her. Asher sat in front of the fire cleaning his rifle while the other two boys whittled. Home. One that Charlotte could see herself a part of, if she wanted to settle down. Which she didn't.

Blinking against the tears stinging her eyes, she turned to clean up the few dishes in the sink. She shouldn't have come. Staying home alone would have been the safest way to spend the day. Not here, seeing the firelight on Asher's light hair, the flames reflections in his eyes. Every time he looked up and grinned, his dimple winking, her resolve to leave the hollow weakened.

Even Matthew's surliness tugged at her heart more than she cared to admit. The two younger boys were sweet as candy when their big brother wasn't coercing them into one of his schemes. How difficult it must be for them all not to know where their father was.

When she'd arrived on Asher's doorstep earlier, he'd handed Charlotte yet another letter from her mother. It rustled from her pocket. She missed her parents desperately, yet had no desire to move back under their roof. She'd had her fill of parties and tea gatherings, picnics and soirees. Teaching gave her life meaning, purpose. Of course, Mother would say that being a wife and mother was purpose enough for a woman.

Maybe it was. Charlotte draped the dish towel over a rod and sat at the table.

"You can be red, Miss Nelson," Luke said, laying out the pieces. "Black is my lucky color. I always win when I play Uncle Asher."

"Do you, now?" Charlotte met Asher's glance over the boy's head. Very well. She could take a hint and was willing to lay aside her competitiveness.

After losing three games in a row and listening to Luke crowing over his victories and Matthew's and Mark's laughter at her losses, Charlotte beat Luke in the fourth game. The fastest game in the history of Plumville, no doubt. She flashed a grin and stood to check the turkey. After all, it wouldn't do for the little scoundrel to win every time, now would it?

Luke pouted and tossed the pieces back in their wooden box. "Luck, that's all. I'm so hungry I couldn't pay attention."

"Sure." Asher tousled his hair. "Losing teaches humility, and you were acting mighty proud over a few games." He peeked in the oven. "Turkey smells good."

"We'll be eating in an hour," Charlotte promised.

"I need to mash these sweet potatoes and snap some beans."

"The boys can snap the beans." Asher waved them over.

"That's woman's work," Matthew complained.

"Yeah, woman's work." Mark crossed his arms in imitation of his brother.

"We don't usually have a woman around here and do this type of thing all the time." Asher plopped the bowl of beans on the table. "Get busy."

Charlotte turned to hide a smile. She'd been wrong about Asher. He had a quiet way of disciplining the boys. Why she'd ever thought he needed to do so openly was beyond her.

"I feel bad that you're doing all the cooking when you're our guest." Asher stepped close, the scent of his shaving soap sending Charlotte's senses whirling.

"I don't mind. At home, I'd most likely be eating a slice of ham on bread." It surprised her to know she really didn't care that she was doing the cooking. When Pastor Sweeney had the same idea, she'd been flooded with irritation and outrage. With Asher, she felt privileged and part of something bigger than herself.

With beans cooked and potatoes mashed, Charlotte put the last dish on the table and stepped back so Asher had room to carve the turkey. She hung her apron on a hook and surveyed the result of a rewarding morning. The turkey, cooked to perfection and golden brown, sat in its juices, ringed with roasted onions. A bowl of mashed yams, sprinkled with brown sugar and pecans sat next to the main dish along with flaky biscuits and green beans. Her mother would be proud. Papa, too, although he wouldn't say much, just give her a wink and dig into the bounty.

"Have a seat, Charlotte." Asher cut into the turkey. "I'll serve from here. Everything looks wonderful. Sit and relax for a while."

"Don't mind if I do." She'd worn her silly dress boots again and her toes protested with a vengeance. What women would do to look pretty for a man. Goodness, she wanted Asher to think her pretty. She wanted him to gush about her cooking.

Her face heated. *Charlotte Nelson, you are a foolish woman, mooning over a mountain sheriff.* She was in danger of throwing away everything she'd worked so hard for. She cut a glance his way, noting that he needed a haircut. She watched the way his strong hands gripped the knife as it sliced into the turkey breast. Her breathing quickened, and she plopped the rest of the way onto her chair.

She was falling hopelessly in love with Asher Thomas.

"Heavenly Father." Asher tried to concentrate on the blessing instead of the way Charlotte's soft hand felt in his. "We thank You for the bounty before us and for the lovely company You've sent to us this day. We ask for a special blessing on Miss Nelson and on the upcoming Christmas pageant. May You soften the hearts of those involved and let them decipher Your will. Amen."

"Amen." Charlotte's gentle response washed across his heart like a salve. She lifted tear-filled eyes to him. "Thank you. That means a lot to me, that you would ask God to help me with the pageant. Does this mean you'll sing?"

Confound the woman. She could grab hold of one thing and hold on like a badger. He sighed and released her hand. "You've convinced me. How about risers for the angel choir? That way, everyone can see them. Or maybe an entire stage, to set the cast higher for those in the back of the building?"

"That's a wonderful idea!" She clapped her hands. "We'll have you sing last. The grand finale. Oh, this will be wonderful."

He was in for sure, now. The three boys grinned at him like simpletons. Since he'd all but forced them to act in the play, it served him right to have to sing. God have mercy. His bite of turkey stuck in his throat. He gasped.

Charlotte leaped to her feet and pounded on his back. "Are you all right? Are you choking? Matthew, get him some water."

"I'm…fine." Asher waved a hand. "Swallowed wrong."

"Oh, good. I thought you were upset about having to sing." She sat back down and spooned a mouthful of yams. After swallowing, she continued. "You aren't, are you? A voice like yours should be heard."

"Maybe we could sing together." Then he could sing low and let her voice carry his.

"No, I can't carry a tune, unfortunately." She smiled. "I love singing, but don't have the gift, I'm afraid."

"Uncle Asher is afraid to sing in public." Matthew waved a biscuit. "Said people laughed at him once in school because he had a stuttering problem."

"Goodness." Charlotte's eyes widened. "I'm sorry for assuming. I've never been good at taking no for an answer."

He couldn't back out now, not after seeing the pleasure on her face. "I don't stutter anymore. Everything will be fine." His hand shook as he buttered his biscuit. "It's time for me to get over this particular phobia."

"God will help you, Asher." She laid a hand on his, taking away any second thoughts he had. Seeing the joy on her face might make singing in public worth it. *Maybe.*

He studied her face and those of his nephews. If his brother should never come home, Asher had all he needed around this table. A beautiful woman he could call friend, if nothing more. Three healthy boys. A family, almost. He shoved aside the thought of Charlotte leaving at the end of spring. That was months away. Anything could happen by then.

"How are preparations for the pageant coming?" Asher tried the turkey again, pleased to discover its tenderness. His choking had nothing to do with the quality of the food and all to do with his fear.

"Better than expected." Charlotte set her napkin beside her plate and frowned. "Folks are still skeptical, but none have refused to allow their children to attend rehearsals. I'm afraid, though, that the audience will be split. How is it that Pastor Sweeney can be so small-minded and yet teach the word of God?"

Asher cleared his throat. "I told you the feud was over a woman, correct?"

"Yes, and Hank Jones told me that if Sweeney backed down, then he would."

"Easier said than done. When the woman took off with a city fella after playing the Joneses and Sweeneys against each other, words were spoken and shots fired. Hank's grandfather was wounded and limped until the day he died." Asher shook his head. "For Hank to be willing to end the feud says a lot about the man's integrity. I've tried to patch things between the two families, but both are stubborn and full of pride. I doubt they even know why they're mad anymore.

"As for Sweeney being a preacher, well, that's a mystery. Folks seem okay with it. Obviously, there is some good in Duke. He's helped lots of folks around here."

"But only on Sunday."

Asher nodded. "Yes. Only on Sunday. If a Jones comes to him with a grievance, he saves it until Sunday to take care of. The only One who can heal Sweeney is God."

"I still don't understand why he's holding on to a grudge after all these years if it was Hank's grandfather who was wounded."

Asher didn't like airing the hollow's dirty laundry, but by filling Charlotte in, maybe he could help her understand the way the hill people thought. "The woman was engaged to Sweeney's grandfather when Old Man Jones started courting her. Both strapping young men, handsome and full of pride. Of course, this was before Sweeney's grandfather married the woman who became Duke's grandmother. It's complicated, but the woman was with child. She lost it over the stress of the two men fighting over her and never would say which of them was the baby's father."

"How sad." Charlotte bowed her head, a bit confused. "So much pain and hatred, but this woman still chose another. She doesn't sound like a woman of good morals. Not someone worth starting a feud over, anyway."

"No, but the heart wants what the heart wants. During a harvest party, punches were thrown. Duke's grandfather was shot, and a Jones was killed. People hold on to anger up here."

"Then I'll pray for every one of them. I'll pray that the story of Christ's birth melts even the hardest of hearts."

"I never knew that somebody died," Matthew said. "I've always wondered about the feud." He set his fork down. "I'm glad we've never gotten into the middle of it. I've got my eye on one of the Jones gals. I'm going to marry her someday."

Charlotte met Asher's glance and laughed. He smirked then joined in. Soon, they all laughed around the table, increasing their laughter when Matthew scowled. Asher reached over and tousled Matthew's hair. "I bet you will, son. I bet you will."

"Maybe we can have a double wedding with you and Miss Nelson." Matthew grinned.

Four days later, Charlotte still reeled from Matthew's seemingly innocent comment about a double wedding. She'd kept her distance from the Thomas family since then. Asher's shocked look, as if the idea abhorred him, was enough to keep any woman away.

Now she stared over a sea of faces eager to begin actual rehearsals after celebrating the Thanksgiving holiday. She took a deep breath and avoided glancing at Matthew Thomas. After all, the boy had simply made a comment out of his youthful naivete, hadn't he? The fact that he might know exactly what he'd said was inconceivable.

Charlotte clapped her hands to get the students' attention. "Today, we will read over our lines in the order of appearance on the stage. Then, we'll move into the songs for our angel choir."

A small girl in the back raised her hand. "Do we get to wear our costumes?"

"Well, I—"

"Georgie has been wearing his ever since you gave

it to him." The girl's lip curled. "And his sister, too. I don't think that's fair to the rest of us."

"Of course it isn't." Charlotte had dug herself into a corner that time. "All I ask is that you keep them clean for the performance." Making sure the Colson children were warm enough would be worth a dirt smudge or two.

The schoolhouse door banged open. Pastor Sweeney barged in and took up his spot against the far wall.

Charlotte turned and rolled her eyes. She'd hoped he'd decided not to join them that afternoon. But since she intended to question him about being a proper shepherd to the Plumville flock, the safest place to do so would be surrounded by children. Then the man could make no inappropriate comments about her qualifications as a wife.

She watched the door, waiting for Asher to make his usual appearance, also. The doorway remained empty of his large form. She didn't know whether to be relieved or saddened.

During the hour of rehearsal, Pastor Sweeney silently stared from his spot, occasionally flicking his glance from Lucy to Frank. Both youngsters wisely kept their focus on the material in front of them. By the time the hour came to an end, Charlotte's nerves were strung as tight as a fiddle. The man's incessant hovering had to end.

"Mr. Sweeney, a word before you leave, if you please." Charlotte helped the smaller students don their outer clothing. Georgie took his sister's hand, flashed Charlotte a grin and dashed out the door, warm in his colorful coat. Charlotte smiled and turned back to the pastor.

The smile on his face alerted her to the fact that he

pleased very much to stay and have a word. Charlotte waved a hand toward one of the desks. "Sit, please. Lucy, please take a seat in the back of the room while I converse privately with your father."

Charlotte took a seat in a desk beside the pastor and ran a hand over the scarred, ink-stained top. "As the pastor of Plumville, you are the person, I believe, to answer some of my questions."

"Absolutely." Sweeney straightened, adopting the somber attitude he usually reserved for Sundays. "How may I help you?"

"It's quite personal, Pastor." Charlotte peeked from under lowered lashes. "And involves you."

"Indeed?" His chest puffed farther.

There was no other way to say what was on her mind except quickly. "I'm concerned with the feud, and wonder how you do it. How do you minister to this town while at constant odds with half of it?"

He leaned forward. "I am still very much a man, Miss Nelson."

She straightened, putting as much distance between them as the desks would allow. "How does that answer my question?"

"I am prone to sin, same as the next." He crossed his arms. "Being a pastor does not make me sinless. Yes, the feud is wrong, but it's been a part of this mountain for so long, I'm not sure any of us knows how to end it."

"A handshake would suffice, Pastor."

"Yes, I can see the situation bothers you greatly." He nodded. "I will pray harder for a solution." He reached across and laid his hand on hers. "Anything that may endear me to you."

She gasped and pulled her hand away. "You can't do this for me. This is something for you."

"I will think on it." He stood, buttoning his dark coat. "This has been on my mind for years."

"Hank Jones says he is willing if you are." Charlotte stood and offered her hand. "I, too, will pray for this foolish feud to end. God can work miracles, as you know." Her heart leaped. Could there finally be an end in sight? Could she dare hope that she might have made a difference in the minds of these mountain people? That this could be the reason God brought her to a one-room schoolhouse?

They had certainly made an impact on her. Gone were Charlotte's selfish ways. Not that she hadn't always desired to care for those less fortunate than herself. But here, in this beautiful place with these proud people, she found life to be more, bigger, than she'd ever known. And she found herself reluctant to leave.

"Good day, Miss Nelson." Pastor Sweeney strode down the aisle between the desks. "Lucy, it's time to go." Together, man and daughter left the building.

Charlotte plopped back into her seat, thankful for the man's response to her question. His answer had been so simple. Hopefully, the solution would be so, too. A simple handshake between the grandsons of two angry and foolish men.

"Teacher, come quick!" Matthew raced inside. "Mr. Colson is hurting Georgie."

Without bothering to grab her coat, Charlotte hefted her skirt and dashed outside and down the path that led through the woods. Mr. Colson's fist was raised for another strike to the boy on the ground. The man glared as Charlotte launched herself at him and grabbed his arm.

"Stop, Mr. Colson. He is only a child." She grappled

with him. He shoved her away. She stumbled, landing in a tangle of skirts.

"Mind your own business, you nosey, no-good woman!" Mr. Colson aimed a kick at her, connecting with her ribs.

"Run, Matthew. Get your uncle." Charlotte struggled to her feet and pulled Georgie to her. "Quickly. Get inside." They raced away, the cursing man chasing them.

"I'll make you sorry you ever meddled." Mr. Colson grabbed for her blouse.

Charlotte felt it rip. Buttons popped. She fought to close the schoolhouse door before he could enter but she was no match for the man's strength. "Out the window, Georgie. I'll handle your father."

The boy's eyes widened, and he gave her a nod before following her directions.

Charlotte backed up, trying to put as much space between her and Mr. Colson as possible. His whiskey-laced breath washed over her. Her stomach churned. Her heart raced. She could never best him physically, and from the look on his face she knew the man was not in a talking mood. When she found the wall at her back, she stiffened and tilted her chin. At least with his focus on her, the children could get away. *Please, God, send them somewhere safe.*

"I've had enough of your interference." Colson seized her chin in a fierce grip. "Filling my boy's head with nonsense of plays and stories." He leaned in closer. "Of God." He raised his fist. "Where is your God now?"

His fist connected with her head. The last thing Charlotte saw before the day went black was the corner of her oak desk and a flicker through her mind of Asher's face.

* * *

"Uncle Asher!" Matthew, followed by his brothers, barreled down the dirt path. "Miss Nelson's in trouble at the school!"

"Get home and wait for me there." Asher spurred his horse into motion. They couldn't go very fast on the narrow trail through the woods and he found himself wanting to run rather than urge the horse to move quicker. Still, the animal's long legs would eat up the distance in a shorter amount of time than Asher could run.

When he reached the school, he leaped from the horse's back before it came to a complete stop. The door to the building hung open. A thin tendril of smoke rose above the stovepipe. "Charlotte?"

Asher pounded up the three steps and inside, squinting against the dimness. Already night was beginning to fall and the room grew frigid. "Charlotte?" She had to be there. There might have been a time or two that she opened the school door late, but he found it hard to figure that she'd fail to lock it closed.

There! A pair of feet stuck from behind her desk, the stockings torn. Asher fell to his knees beside her, taking in with one glance the disheveled hair and torn clothes. A purple lump marred the side of her forehead. The paleness of her face yanked at his heart, sending it into an irregular rhythm. He leaned closer. Praise God, she still breathed.

He removed his coat and wrapped it around her. Taking her home wouldn't be proper. He'd take her to the Widow Slater's, then call for the herb woman.

Climbing on his horse with an unconscious woman took a bit of skill, but after laying Charlotte across first, then climbing on and pulling her back into his arms,

Asher managed. He kept her cradled close as he turned for the widow's.

What had happened to her? Who in this hollow would harm the teacher? His gut tightened, remembering the sight of her torn clothing. Please, God, don't let her have been ravished. Not sweet, caring Charlotte.

Keeping Charlotte in his arms, he flung a leg over and slid from the horse.

"Mr. Thomas?" Widow Slater stood in her doorway, outlined with light from her fire. "Mercy, what happened?" She rushed forward and smoothed Charlotte's hair away from her face.

"I found her at the school like this."

"Bring her inside. I've a cot against the far wall you can lay her on."

"Thank you, Leah." Proprieties be hanged. If the woman would help him with Charlotte, then Asher counted her friend.

Leah held a lantern high while Asher unwrapped Charlotte. She gasped. "Was she…?"

"I don't know. I don't think so." His throat burned and he buried his face in his hands. "I need to go for the herb woman. Will you care for her?"

Leah placed a hand on his arm and peered up into his face. "You love this woman?"

He nodded. "But she's leaving at the end of spring."

"Go. I'll get her undressed and warmed up. Hurry, though. I don't like the sound of her breathing or the fact she hasn't woken on the ride from the school." All business now, Leah turned her back to him.

Asher knew from the look on her face that the widow now knew there was no chance between the two of them, yet she didn't hesitate to help another in need.

As he raced away, he prayed God would send a good man for Leah.

By the time he located Mrs. Mahoney, dark had fully fallen. What if Charlotte had slipped into death while he was gone? He'd never be able to get into another sparring match with her or watch the sparks flash from her beautiful eyes. He rubbed his hands across his face. He couldn't think like that.

She'd be sitting up in bed, alarmed at all the fuss. He stopped in front of Leah's cabin and helped Mrs. Mahoney dismount before dragging the poor woman inside.

Leah turned. "She hasn't moved."

"Step aside." Mrs. Mahoney knelt beside the cot. "Wait outdoors, Sheriff."

His shoulders slumped. He wanted to stay, but of course Charlotte would need to be examined. Tongues would wag if he stayed. He stepped outside and stared at the star-filled sky, lifting prayers for Charlotte's health heavenward. Making promises to God that he hoped he could keep.

He'd stop searching for his brother who didn't wish to be found and focus instead on the three children under his roof. He'd work harder at stopping the silly feud. Anything, if God spared Charlotte's life.

Chapter 11

After three days of unconsciousness, and one day nursed by Leah Slater, Charlotte was eager to get back home and to teaching. Asher hadn't been there when she'd awoken, but Leah had gushed for hours about how long he'd stayed by her bedside, praying for her to wake up. Unfortunately, a dispute on the mountain had called him away from her. Weakened from her ordeal, waking up and not seeing him there brought her to tears.

"Are you in pain?" Leah brought her a cup of tea. "I've some medicine."

"No, thank you. Just a bit weepy. It'll pass."

"Asher should return this evening, and he'll be full of questions for you." Leah pulled up a chair. "Matthew said it was Mr. Colson who struck you?"

"Matthew saw?" Charlotte clutched the neckline of her borrowed nightgown. No child should see such horror. She released the lace at her throat and felt the receding bump on her head.

"No, he didn't actually see, I don't think, but he did tell his uncle later that Mr. Colson was beating Georgie and that you were in trouble."

"Is that where Asher has gone? To confront Mr. Colson?"

Leah shook her head. "He tried, but the man is nowhere to be found."

"Who's watching the children?" Charlotte swung her legs off the side of the cot. "They can't be left out there alone."

"And you can't take care of them. Not right now." Leah placed her legs back on the bed and took her mug. "Rest. We'll tell Asher of your concerns when he returns, although, to the man's credit, I'm sure he's already found homes for the poor children."

She was right. Asher wouldn't allow the two little ones to stay alone. Charlotte lay back with a sigh. She'd nap for a few hours, and when nightfall came, she'd sneak out and go home. A girl couldn't impose on someone for too long, and Charlotte had never made a good patient.

At home, she could work on lessons, mending and sewing her new Christmas dress. Scores of projects needed her attention. Here, she could find nothing to do but count the knots in the wood above her head.

What if Mother should find out about the attack? She'd demand Charlotte return home immediately. But she couldn't hold the information from her parents. She needed to find a way of telling her mother about her injury, once she was fully recovered, of course, and minimize the details.

A pounding sounded on the door along with raised voices. Charlotte sat up and pulled the quilt to her chin.

Hank Jones and Pastor Sweeney crowded into the cabin the instant Leah opened her door. They removed their hats and marched to Charlotte's cot.

"We heard someone done hit you a few times. Busted up some ribs," Hank said. "We also heard tell it was Ben Colson. Now, we want you to come clean and tell us if it's so. We want to set the man straight."

Charlotte glanced from one man to the other, not sure how to respond. On one hand, the fact they wanted to work together warmed her heart. On the other, she knew the anger and grudges these two men were willing to carry to their grave. "Oh, no, gentlemen. We were having a civilized conversation and, well, I must admit that I'm a bit clumsy and fell."

Hank's brows lowered. "Did he threaten you if you told the truth?" He glanced at Duke. "He's more rotten than I suspected, if our teacher will lie for the man."

Duke pulled aside his coat. "Tell us truthfully, Miss Nelson. The folks of this town take care of their own, and we don't abide our womenfolk being abused."

Tears spilled from her eyes. Their own! The people of Plumville claimed her as one of them.

"Now look what you've done, Pastor! She's crying." Hank took a step back. "Mrs. Slater, come help."

Charlotte waved a hand. "No, it's the fact that you care that has me weeping."

"I'm confused." Hank twisted his hat. "Duke, you got an older daughter. You understand any of this?"

"The ways of a woman are a mystery, Hank." Sweeney shook his head. "I fear Miss Nelson may be on her last leg and will soon be joining God Almighty."

"For goodness' sake." Leah shoved between them

then turned to usher them out the door. "Get out of here, you fools." She giggled and batted her eyes at the pastor.

Hmm. Quite possibly the woman had transferred her attention from Asher to Duke, Charlotte thought. The gesture wasn't lost on him, either. He smiled and allowed her to usher them outside.

The Lord did work in mysterious ways. Charlotte grinned. If being punched pulled the town together, then she would almost welcome another one. She took a deep breath, her wrapped ribs pinching her.

Almost.

"She's sleeping," Leah whispered.

Asher removed his hat and hung it on a hook. "Then I won't wake her." He sighed. "No sign of Ben or the children."

"Do you think he's taken them and moved away?" Leah helped him out of his coat. "Duke and Hank stopped by this afternoon riled to the point of distraction at Charlotte's injuries. I fear the men will do something stupid."

Asher paused on his way to Charlotte's bedside. "They were here together?"

"Yep, and not a cross word to each other. It's amazing."

"It sure is." He moved to Charlotte's cot and noticed her watching him. He pulled a chair close and sat down, taking her hand in his. "Are you all right, Charlie?"

Tears shimmered in her eyes. "The Colson children are missing?"

"It's possible Ben has them." Since he'd failed to get a sharp retort in response to the nickname he'd called her, Asher feared she might not be recovering as quickly as they all hoped.

"But you don't think so."

"No, I don't." He straightened, wishing he could take back his honest answer, wanting nothing more than to wipe away her fears, gather her in his arms and take her home with him. "Ben hasn't been seen since your attack. It's possible he waited in the woods and waylaid the children, but I don't think so. I stopped by his place, but can't tell if anything is missing or not."

"Georgie's coat?"

"That is nowhere to be seen." He smiled. "I can't imagine that boy leaving that coat behind for any reason."

Leah handed him a mug of coffee then moved to help Charlotte sit up. Charlotte waved her off. "I'm fine, thank you. If you have a robe I can borrow, I'd like to get out of this bed and sit in a chair."

"If you're sure." Leah grabbed a thick robe from her bed in the corner.

Asher turned around while Charlotte donned it. "I'll keep looking for them, but figure they're all miles away by now. If I get my hands on that Ben—"

"You'll do absolutely nothing."

He turned at Charlotte's strict words. "What?"

"The man is distraught and fighting demons we can only imagine. You'll leave him alone other than making sure the children are safe. They should be removed from his care, but I'm not going to cause a fuss about the man striking me." She marched to the kitchen table and sat down, pouring herself a cup of coffee.

He stomped to a seat across from her, noticing Leah grab her shawl and head discreetly outside. Smart woman. "You must have hit your head harder than I thought to warrant three days of a deep sleep. Ben Colson should be punished."

"Not if I insist otherwise." She lifted her mug and peered over the rim. "I want you to stop Duke and Hank from doing anything about this."

"What if Ben comes back? I told you there was speculation he killed his wife. That it wasn't an accident."

Her hands trembled, causing some of her drink to slosh over onto the table. "My safety is in God's hands."

Asher slapped the tabletop. "Of all the insane, foolish women I've had the misfortune of meeting, you, Charlotte Nelson, beat them all! I've half a mind to write your mother."

"You wouldn't dare." She narrowed her eyes. "That would unleash a force not even you are capable of dealing with."

"You have no idea what I'm capable of." He jerked to his feet. After suffering such a brutal attack, how could she not desire justice? "It's too late to stop Duke and Hank. I won't need to do a thing."

"Then you'd best go after them, don't you think?" She reached for a biscuit and began buttering it. "You know as well as I how feuds get going in this town. I won't be the cause of another one."

"You're already the cause of this dispute." He ran his hands through his hair. "Maybe not on purpose, but you are." Couldn't she see? The townspeople had accepted her. They'd stop at nothing to avenge her. "You may leave in the spring, anyway. What does it matter whether Ben gets what's coming to him?" He wanted to yank the words out of the air and swallow them when tears spilled down her cheeks. He fell to his knees beside her chair. "I'm sorry. I didn't mean it."

"But you're right, Asher. Why should I care?" She ducked her head. "But I do. I care about everyone here. I care about you."

He pulled her to him, her mussed curls tickling his neck. Cupping her face, he met her eyes, then lowered his lips to hers, savoring their softness.

She exhaled softly then returned his kiss, not with timidity, but with confidence and passion. He deepened the kiss, tightening his hold around her. As if realizing they were alone, she pulled away, brushing her fingertips across her lips.

"We shouldn't, Asher." She moved back to the cot and turned her back to him.

She was right. In too short a time, she'd leave him. Off to follow a silly dream when everything she needed stood right there. He took a step toward her, intending to make her see things the way he did. That they could have something beautiful. Instead, he grabbed his hat and stormed out the door.

After crying herself to sleep and refusing to acknowledge Leah's silent presence, Charlotte sneaked from her cot. Her own clothes were nowhere to be seen so she stuck her feet into her boots, wrapped the bedclothes tightly around her and slipped into the night.

She dashed home and dressed in her own warm clothing. She'd return Leah's things once she located Georgie and Molly. She glanced out the window toward the school. Had anyone thought to look there? The one place the two children felt the safest?

Leaving her door open, Charlotte raced to the school and barged through the door. Smoke greeted her in a gray haze, hovering around the ceiling like a cloud. Huddled next to the stove were the children.

Charlotte hurried to open a couple of windows. "Closing the flue is never a good idea."

Georgie ran and threw his arms around her waist. "You're alive. You came."

"Of course I came." She held out her other arm to invite Molly to join them. "And it takes more than a bump on the head to kill me. Teachers are tough, you know." She knelt and stared into their dirty faces. "You've scared the dickens out of everyone. The sheriff has been looking for you for days. Have you eaten?"

Georgie nodded. "We've been taking food from your place. That's all right, isn't it?"

She grabbed them close. "Of course it is. But now, let's get you back to my cabin and get a hot meal in you." After banking the fire, she ushered the children to her cabin. Relief at finding them unharmed left her knees weak. Not as much as Asher's kiss, but that was something she refused to dwell on. The children needed her.

Tomorrow, she'd have to face Asher Thomas and tell him Georgie and Molly were staying with her until a more permanent home could be found. Her heart almost stopped at the thought. Not only had she sneaked out of Leah's home in the middle of the night, but she'd turned her back on Asher's kisses.

She ran her finger over her lips and closed her eyes, remembering the feel and taste of him. Why couldn't she stay in Plumville and accept what he offered her? She'd find no finer man in Savannah. Her parents would grow to love him.

Opening her eyes, her glance fell on Georgie and Molly. The faces of her other students filtered through her mind. She'd miss all of them. If she married, she could no longer be their teacher, but she could watch them grow into strong mountain men and women.

Watch children of her own roam the fertile hills and

valleys. Dare she allow herself to change the dream she'd carried with her from childhood? Could God have something completely different, better, planned for her?

Something that involved a man named Asher Thomas?

With Georgie and Molly safely ensconced at Leah Slater's cabin for the afternoon, Charlotte unlocked the door to the schoolhouse. She disliked working on a Sunday afternoon, but after missing several days of teaching because of the attack, and worry over the Colson children, she needed to prepare for the next week's lessons and rehearsals.

Several of the students approached her at church, letting her know they'd continued memorizing their lines without formal rehearsal times. If only their parents were so diligent. Charlotte sighed. After Duke's and Hank's visit while she recovered at Leah's, she'd held out hope of reconciliation between the two families. Instead, church that morning had been just as separate as always, slicing through her hope for the town as effectively as Asher's cold glances had cut through her heart.

Although Asher had still stood beside her in the back of the sanctuary, Charlotte could feel his hurt and anger. Pain over her response to his kiss and anger that she'd gone looking for the Colson children on her own. Never mind that he'd agreed the children could stay with her until a long-term home could be found for them. After all, as he'd reminded Charlotte, she had intentions to leave Plumville in a few months.

She banged the door open, not caring that it slammed the wall and made drawings flutter to the floor. Charlotte sighed. It wouldn't do for her mood to spoil what could be a very productive afternoon.

After picking up the students' work, Charlotte placed the papers on her desk and sat down in her chair. If she kept pen to pad, she could plan the lessons by suppertime.

An hour later, hand cramping and back aching, Charlotte lifted her head from her work. Did she smell smoke? She sniffed and glanced at the window. What she saw chilled her to the core. Flames licked the frame of the schoolhouse. Mercy. She grabbed her cloak and raced for the door. She lifted the latch and pushed, but it wouldn't open.

Her heart raced. Perspiration broke out on her forehead, despite the wintry day. Why would the door be bolted from the outside? Someone wanted her to die. Her stomach plummeted. To burn inside the place she taught the town's children. Smoke filtered through charred holes in the wall. She'd been so immersed in her work she hadn't paid attention to her surroundings. This could be a fatal mistake.

She knew without a doubt that Ben Colson was behind this latest attempt toward her. This time, she might not be so forgiving, if she lived. There had to be a way out. *Think, Charlotte.* She couldn't wait for rescue like before. This time, she'd succumb to smoke inhalation before her head hit the desk. Then, she'd burn to a crisp like a slice of bacon.

She coughed, then pulled her handkerchief from her skirt to cover her nose and mouth. The windows were not an option. Already curtains of orange and yellow filled them.

She'd never see Asher again! Or the boys. Or her students.

Stop panicking. She sent a short prayer to God, then

tried to take a deep breath and gagged. Her heart raced. *Focus.* She studied the room through tear-filled eyes.

The back wall. Charlotte dropped to the floor and crawled to the weak spot in the building's siding behind her desk. She'd forgotten to have the Swiss-cheese boards replaced, even after shivering at her desk each day when a frigid breeze found its way inside.

She planted both feet on the wall and kicked. Hard. Then again. One foot went through, then the other. Heedless of the splintered wood, she tore at the boards until her fingers bled, and she'd made a hole large enough to squeeze through. Praise the Lord, the fire had started at the windows. The back wall hadn't caught yet. The roof rained down showers of sparks.

Scuttling free of the building, Charlotte lay and took in deep cleansing breaths. She needed to alert the town. There wasn't time to dally. If she hurried to the church and rang the bell, folks would come.

She looked up at the schoolhouse. Already the roof was engulfed in flames. It was beyond saving. Still, the citizens needed to know what had transpired. That once again, someone tried to harm their teacher. But why? All she wanted to do was help. She tried hard not to force her beliefs on others, and when she did, was quick to back down when asked or told to mind her own business.

She'd never contemplated harming another. Yet, someone had no qualms about leaving her for dead.

Getting to her feet took more effort than she'd thought. She coughed until she feared she'd cough up a lung. How would she make it to the church before the fire spread? Running was out of the question. She stumbled in the direction of the steeple, rising above the tree line. On a good day, the walk would require fifteen minutes, longer when every breath she took cut deep. She'd be too late to do any good.

After a harrowing twenty-minute walk, she stumbled into the churchyard and cried out, reaching a hand toward Asher.

He and Duke turned, then Asher dashed to her side. "Charlotte? What happened?"

"Someone...set fire...to the school. With me inside." She sagged into his arms. Oh, he felt so strong. So safe. "I broke free."

"Your hands." Asher lifted her. "Duke, ring the bell. We need every able-bodied man we can get." He carried her into the church and laid her on one of the polished pews.

"So this is what one of the pews feels like."

"Lie still. I'm getting some water to wash your hands."

"They do burn a bit." She grabbed the back of the seat and tried to pull herself to a sitting position. Pain shot through her fingers. She held her hands in front of her face, and grimaced. Torn and bloody fingernails. Scorched skin.

No help for it. When Charlotte returned to Savannah, she'd wear gloves.

Asher handed her a bowl of water and a rag. "The men are arriving." He cast her an apologetic glance. "I need to be out there."

"I can manage." She waved him away. "Don't let them leave yet. There's something I need to say."

"Isn't there always?" He smiled, his face reflecting sadness. "I'll send a woman in to help you."

"No need. I can manage." The water burned when she plunged her hands into its cool depths. She hissed through her teeth. Maybe she couldn't manage. With both hands damaged, she couldn't bandage. Not with the pain, anyway. She expelled a deep breath and stood to move outside.

Once on the top step of the church, she yelled to get the group's attention. Ten men turned toward her, shovels and buckets in hand. "Gentlemen! Before you go… Hank, Duke, please step forward." She might be behaving in a heavy-handed way, but enough was enough. "The two of you were willing to set aside your differences once before when I needed help."

"Yes, ma'am." Hank glanced at Duke. "And we're willing this time."

Charlotte tilted her head. "The children of Plumville have worked very hard at memorizing their lines and writing poems to read at the pageant. Don't you think their hard work should be rewarded by the laying aside of this silly feud?

"On that first Christmas morning, God gave the world a wonderful gift. The gift of His Son. A gift of His love and mercy. Don't your children deserve the same type of gift from their fathers?" Her voice broke, choked off by sobs caught in her throat. "Do you want them to carry on a grudge that has nothing personally to do with them?"

"We haven't really thought of it that way," Duke admitted. "But, Miss Nelson, there's a fire to fight."

"In a moment. By now there's nothing left of the school, so a few more minutes won't make any difference." She held her hands loosely at her sides and tried to ignore the throbbing in her fingers. "Not only has this feud affected your families, but it's affected the entire town. On Sundays, people must either choose a side or they must stand in the back. I'll stand no more, gentlemen, nor will I choose a side. I will sit in the first empty seat I see and don't care whether it's on the Jones side or the Sweeney side."

Hank glanced to where smoke rose above the trees, black against the gray winter sky. "Fire's burning itself out."

"Are you listening to me, Mr. Jones?"

"Yes, ma'am. Just don't want the woods to burn down."

Charlotte closed her eyes and counted to ten before opening them again and speaking. "Do you know what I want for Christmas?"

The two men shook their heads.

"I want the two of you to shake hands like brothers and let this go." With a swish of her skirts, she moved back inside.

Asher had kept silent during Charlotte's impassioned speech, but now he stepped onto the top step in her place. "I agree with Miss Nelson. For years, I've tried to stop this silly argument. From now on, I'll arrest the next fool who throws a punch. This pageant will go on. With the school burned, it'll take place here, in the church, and the citizens of this town will sit mingled, not separated. If the only people attending are me and Miss Nelson, then we'll sit and bask in God's glory and sing hymns. One way or the other, this pageant will take place."

"Can we go take care of the fire now?" Hank slapped his hat against his leg. "We've heard every word you and the schoolmarm said, but I, for one, need time to think on it."

"That sounds like a wise decision." Duke nodded. "I, too, will spend time in prayer."

"All right, men, let's go assess the damage." Asher

grabbed a shovel of his own and sprinted for his horse. With it being a windless day, they most likely wouldn't even need to save the trees around the clearing. The fire would have burned itself out by now.

When they reached the school yard, Asher took one look at the smoldering pile of what used to be the schoolhouse and decided first thing he'd do would be to hunt down Ben Colson and knock out some of the man's teeth.

Not that Charlotte had said anything about the fire being set on purpose. She didn't need to. One look at the building, the charred plank used to block the door and the empty kerosene lantern told him all he needed to know.

"Sheriff!" one of the men called to him from the edge of the forest. "You might want to come have a look."

Asher dropped his shovel and trotted over. Ben Colson lay among the dried leaves, an empty whiskey bottle in his hand and blood pooling under his head. The blue color to his lips told Asher the man was dead, but he felt for a breath, anyway. Nothing.

He tried to drum up even a small measure of compassion for the fool, but all he saw was Charlotte's burned and bloody hands. The three days she lay unconscious after his first attack. God forgive him, but Asher couldn't feel sorry for the drunken menace. "Someone needs to take him home. We'll bury him next to his wife."

"Poor young'uns." Hank stepped up and removed his hat. "I ain't got much, Sheriff, but I'll take the young'uns if you want me to."

Asher clapped the man on the shoulder. "The Widow Slater has them now. There's no rush to find them a home, but I appreciate the offer. You've a good heart, Hank."

"So you're singing at the pageant?"

"I reckon so." Asher scratched his eyebrow. "Did you ever think the day would come?"

"Not after the fiasco when we were in school." Hank bumped him with his shoulder. "You did stutter something awful back then. Sorry I laughed at you."

"Just kids being kids." Asher slapped his hat back on his head. "I'm heading back to check on Miss Nelson."

"That woman sure does get into some scrapes. Not sure how she's managed to live to see adulthood."

Asher laughed. Leave it to Hank to lighten up a somber mood. "You're right at that."

He returned to an empty church, and knew without being told that Charlotte had gone to the widow's place for help.

Plopping into the nearest pew, he let his gaze rest on the simple cross adorning the far wall. If Asher asked, would God grant him his desire to have Charlotte as his wife? Maybe that wasn't part of God's plan. Maybe Charlotte was only in Plumville to heal its people and let Asher know that his heart was ready to love a woman. That he could set aside his job and come home to a family in the evenings. He could accept that. Especially with the realization that his brother was probably gone for good, and Asher would have full responsibility for the boys.

Still, the woman he wanted to come home to was Charlotte.

Chapter 12

Charlotte stood, bandaged hands on the shoulders of Georgie and Molly, and stared into the hole dug for their father. A simple pine coffin, hurriedly constructed from rough lumber, lay at the bottom. The pastor spoke on the effects of hatred and the damage it did to the one who harbored it and those around that person. Charlotte prayed the people around her listened to his words, especially the pastor. He was guilty of the very thing he preached against.

Since her bossy speech on the church steps, no mention of the feud had reached her ears. Dare she hope they'd put it behind them? She had yet to see a handshake between Hank and Duke. Maybe that was too much to ask. She should be happy with peace between the families. She'd know as soon as she stepped into church on Sunday.

Molly's thin shoulders shook under Charlotte's hand,

transferring Charlotte's attention to the grieving children. As the first clods of dirt were tossed into the grave, she turned them toward her cabin.

"I've soup warming on the stove. Let's get out of the cold."

Georgie pulled free. "I want to stay for a few more minutes. Pa shouldn't be alone right now. Not until the last shovelful is dropped."

"Then we'll wait with you." Charlotte turned back to watch as the hole was filled. Her heart ached for the children. As abusive a man as Ben Colson had been, he was their father and they loved him. Hank had kindly offered to take them in, but Charlotte wasn't ready to let go of her role as foster parent. She would soon. In plenty of time for them to adjust to their new home before she left Plumville.

"Some of the ladies got together a potluck at the church," Asher said, coming to stand beside them. "It was last minute. No need to bring anything."

"That's very thoughtful of them." Charlotte thought about her pot of soup. Not much, but she wouldn't arrive empty-handed.

"Why?" Georgie scowled. "No one cared about my pa. He was a mean drunk. Everybody said so often enough."

Asher laid a hand on the boy's head. "Even so, folks did care, and now they care about you and your sister. Don't throw their good intentions in their faces."

He shrugged. "I won't eat a bite, but I'll go." He whirled and stomped away.

"Is there cake?" Molly asked. "I haven't had cake in a long time."

"I'm sure there is." Charlotte blinked back tears and

looked at Asher, who nodded. "Go get yourself a big piece, sweetheart. I'll follow behind with Mr. Thomas."

"Will you resume rehearsals tomorrow?" Asher asked, matching his steps to hers.

"Yes. I believe the children need a semblance of normality, not to mention that Christmas is two weeks away. We still have much to do." She stopped and faced him. "Thank you for all your help. I'm not sure the townspeople would have come around and accepted me and my mad idea of a pageant without you."

His mouth twitched. "I think they saw right to your heart, Charlotte Nelson. They know you have only their children's best intentions in mind."

Did he see right to her heart? Could he see how difficult the thought of leaving was becoming? It was hard enough with her growing feelings for him, but now there were two children who needed her, not counting his three motherless nephews.

What would he do if she told him she wanted to stay? What if she tossed all propriety to the wind and proposed marriage to him? Maybe she would.

"I'm sure I could come up with something else to knock these people off their foundations." She grinned and slipped her arm through his, enjoying the look of shock on his face.

He chuckled. "I'm sure you could. This place will never be the same after meeting Charlotte Nelson."

She planned on it. "Who will you have to save every day once I'm gone? Life will become very boring."

"I'm sure the boys will more than make up for your shenanigans." They'd reached the church, and Asher slipped free. "I'm going to grab a quick bite to eat, then get started on that platform I promised you."

"You might want to practice your singing, too?" Charlotte winked and dashed into the building.

Little minx. Asher couldn't figure her out if his life depended on it. One moment she held herself aloof, the next she treated him as a lifelong friend, hanging on his arm as if it were the most natural thing in the world. He shook his head. He didn't want to be her friend. He wanted much more.

He shivered in his coat, wishing the potluck was somewhere warmer than the churchyard. The ground crunched under his feet from the previous night's freeze. Few remnants of snow lingered, except for isolated patches under thick bushes. There'd be snow for Christmas, though, unless the mountain chose to be different this year.

Molly sat under a leafless oak tree, her fist full of chocolate cake. Georgie must have changed his mind about eating because he sat next to his sister with a fried chicken leg in each hand.

The Jones family was to be commended for offering to take the Colson children into their home, but Asher knew they already struggled to provide food and clothing for their own offspring. No, he'd have to find another home for the Colson children after Charlotte left. He spied Leah strolling across the yard. She'd make a good mother for them, and made an honest living off the dresses she made and sent to the city on consignment. Someday, she'd have her own dress shop.

Charlotte emerged from the church sanctuary, and all Asher's bright ideas flew on the wind. She would make somebody a wonderful wife. Some children a loving mother. He shoved his hands in his pockets and turned the other way, not wanting to ponder something that left his heart cold, knowing he couldn't have her.

A man came toward him, thin and wearing no coat. Asher squinted, trying to make out his features. He looked familiar, the long-legged gait similar to Asher's own. He caught his breath and stared until he was sure.

"Leroy!" He held himself from running to his brother and planting a right hook alongside his head. Instead, he rushed to gather the man in a hug. "Where have you been?"

Leroy's teeth flashed under his thick beard. "Well, I spent some time in jail for robbing a stagecoach, found Jesus while I was there, then headed up north to do some logging to pay off my debts. Paid off the folks I robbed. Now I'm home." He pulled free of Asher's hug. "You look good, little brother. Real good. Where's my boys?"

"Behind the church, stuffing their faces with food." Leroy spent time in jail? Asher shook his head. With him being sheriff around these parts, someone should've told him. "Where were you in jail?"

"Virginia. But I've left those ways behind me now. I'm ready to be a father." Leroy glanced around. "Who died?"

"Ben Colson." Asher loved his brother, but he'd believe he'd changed when he saw the evidence firsthand.

Leroy clapped Asher on the shoulder. "No great loss. May God have mercy on his soul. We'll catch up later. Right now I have some rascals to hug." He hurried around the corner of the church.

Within seconds, whooping and hollering filled the somber air. Asher smiled at the joyful sounds, his heart torn between relief at his brother coming home, and melancholy over the boys moving back to their father's cabin. His gaze fell again on Georgie and Molly. Without children, his cabin would be mighty lonesome.

"Your brother is home." Charlotte's eyes sparkled.

He hadn't heard her approach. "Yep. Those three boys will be wilder than ever."

"Maybe their actions were a direct result of their father's absence, and they'll settle down now."

"Quite possibly." He hadn't thought of it that way.

The boys could have felt abandoned and unloved, and acting ornery garnered them much-needed attention. Well, Asher had fallen short in that area until a few months ago. Until a raven-haired, blue-eyed, sassy girl from Georgia arrived on his doorstep and taught him the error of his ways and what a complete family could feel like.

Leroy and the boys walked their way, Luke tugging at his daddy's hand. "This is our teacher, Pa. Her name is Miss Nelson, and she's the best teacher ever!"

"She is?" Leroy winked. "She's mighty purty, too."

Luke frowned. "Teachers ain't pretty. She's making us be wise men in her play. Uncle Asher is going to sing."

"He is?" Leroy sent a questioning look Asher's way.

Asher shrugged, tempted to change his mind if his singing was going to send everybody upside down. And with the admiring glance Leroy bestowed on Charlotte, Asher needed to squash the interest right there. "Well, when a pretty gal asks, what's a man to say? Besides, Miss Nelson will be leaving in the spring. We might as well make her stay as memorable as possible."

"I get the hint, brother." Leroy grinned. "Come on, boys. Let's get your things and head over to our own place and get a fire started."

"Mr. Thomas." Uh-oh. Asher recognized the determined glint in Charlotte's eyes. "I'm sure your cabin is uninhabitable after your long absence. Maybe it would be wiser for you to stay with your brother for a few more days until you and the boys have time to clean."

His amused gaze met Asher's. "You've got your hands full, don't you?"

Asher wished.

Charlotte clapped her hands, now free of bandages. Other than a few scars, which she prayed would fade in time, they were as good as new. "Children! It's December twenty-second, our dress rehearsal. Tomorrow is our show. I know you're as excited as I am, but we have so much to do." She feared they wouldn't be ready. Rehearsals had been sporadic at best, especially with all the misfortunes that had befallen her lately, and half the students had yet to arrive. She glanced at the sanctuary door. She shouldn't have let them go home for supper first, but children usually behaved better on full stomachs.

At least Duke hadn't arrived to oversee things. He seemed resigned to the fact that Lucy would play opposite Frank.

She glanced at Georgie and Molly dancing in their costumes. A few angels milled around, crawling under the pews and mussing their white robes. Lucy and Frank gazed puppy-eyed at each other, daring to share a pew since Duke wasn't around. Where were the Thomas boys? She needed them to help her move the pulpit to stage left.

With a sigh, she flattened her back against the solid oak podium and braced her feet. Grunting, she pushed. The podium tottered, then fell with a crash. Oh, no, what had she done? She tried to lift it and noticed the broken corner. She'd be run out of town for sure!

"That can be sanded down, Miss Nelson," Georgie assured her.

"I hope so." She needed to gather her wits before she destroyed something else. Squeezing between the two lovebirds, Charlotte focused her attention on the cross hanging above them. She closed her eyes and took deep breaths, letting God's spirit settle her. The air was filled with the scents of evergreen and beeswax candles. The children's chatter lowered to a murmur. Little by little the tension started to leave Charlotte's shoulders.

"Teacher?" Lucy shook her.

"Shhh."

"Miss Nelson?" Frank leaned close enough for her to feel his breath on her cheek. "Perhaps the strain has been too much for her. Should I run for the sheriff?"

"There's no need for that." Charlotte opened one eye. "I insist you give me a moment."

"A moment for what?" Frank's brow furrowed. "Oh, you're praying. Lucy, fetch your pa."

"For goodness' sake." Charlotte smoothed her hair. "I do not need the sheriff or the pastor. I need a moment to gather my thoughts so we can proceed with the rehearsal." And she needed to figure out what to do with the broken podium. "Frank, please see if you can set the podium up and scoot it to its assigned location. Lucy, gather the younger children. We'll proceed without the others. All the major players are here." She should have delegated to begin with, instead of trying to run things completely on her own.

"I don't think the Joneses are coming," Lucy explained. "Frank told me his little sister has colic."

Not the baby Jesus. Could anything else go wrong

with the program? "Frank, where are your other siblings?"

"They can't come unless they walk with me and they
weren't ready in time. I didn't want to be late." With a
great heave, he set the podium upright. "Uh, Teacher,
there's a crack running down the side of this."

"Can you face it away from the congregation?"

"It's a big crack, ma'am."

"Then we'll drape fabric over it for tomorrow, and
I'll pay to have a new one built." Charlotte buried her
face in her hands. God help her get through the next
two days. Taking another deep breath, though at this
rate she'd pass out from hyperventilation, she grabbed
her Bible off the brand-new platform and turned to the
Gospel of Luke. "Everyone, take your places. We'll
walk through this a couple of times. Other than the wise
men, the missing actors are minor." Oh, she'd ring the
Thomas men's necks.

The sanctuary doors banged open and the tardy wise
men barged in. She narrowed her eyes. "You're very
late, gentlemen."

"Sorry." Matthew glanced at Mark. "You forgot our
costumes."

"No, I told Luke to carry them."

The youngest Thomas brother stared wide-eyed.
"But Uncle Asher told us to run or he'd be late picking up his package, and Pa's busy fixing the roof on
our cabin."

Charlotte closed her eyes and rolled her neck. "Never
mind. At least you're here. Please do not forget them
tomorrow. Take your places."

The children thundered into place, tripping over
the steps of the platform and almost knocking over the
crudely constructed stable. Charlotte shook her head.

"Unto us is born this day in the city of... Matthew, stop shoving your brother."

"He pushed me first."

"Did not." Mark gave him another push.

"Enough!" Charlotte stomped her foot. "We only have tonight and tomorrow to get through. I'm sure the three of you can cooperate for that long. If not, you'll be writing your sums after Christmas until your fingers fall off. Are we clear?"

"Yes, ma'am," they said in unison, hanging their heads.

"Very good."

"Let's start again. Unto us is born—"

By the time rehearsal was finished, Charlotte's head pounded, and she had given up all hope for a success-ful pageant. Once the costumes were removed from the children and neatly folded on a pew, Charlotte wrapped Georgie and Molly in a spare cloak of hers and sent the other students home. At that moment, she wanted noth-ing more than to sit in front of the fire with a nice cup of tea the moment the children were down for the night.

"Time for bed," she announced, pushing open the door to her cabin. Welcome warmth from the low-burning embers greeted her. She couldn't wait to kick off her boots and slip her feet into rabbit-fur slippers.

Asher burrowed deeper into his coat, wondering what his passengers were thinking as they silently watched the dark scenery slip past. Light snowflakes drifted down, making the night glow. Occasionally, he'd hear a whisper too low for him to make out the words. Why they'd written to the sheriff to come fetch them was a mystery. They could have hired a driver easy enough. But it was Christmas, and he was glad to help out.

He wasn't sure where they'd spend the night. Most of the mountain cabins had little space for visitors, and the one where they headed already stretched at the seams. He chuckled, envisioning Charlotte's reaction when she saw them. What a gift. He'd only wished they could have surprised her during rehearsal.

"How much farther, Sheriff?" The woman's Southern accent washed over him as soft as a southern rain. So like Charlotte's, he actually turned to see who it was he answered.

"No more than an hour, ma'am."

"I've never been so cold." She shuddered and placed glove-covered hands over her nose.

"There's another blanket under the seat. You're welcome to it."

"No, thank you. It smells of horses."

Asher grinned. That was exactly what he'd used it for last. "I'll get us there as fast as possible."

"Oh, Henry," the woman sighed. "She'll be asleep when we arrive."

"No worry, Bernadette. She'll be glad to wake when she sees you." He put his arm around his wife.

"I still say we should have written." She laid her head on her husband's shoulder. "Are you married, Mr. Thomas?"

"No, ma'am, but I've got my eye on a certain young lady." He hoped the arrival of her parents wouldn't be the last straw to convince her to return to Savannah. Plumville wouldn't be the same if she did.

"Is my daughter in good health? Some of her letters seemed…a bit sparse concerning how well she was doing. Instead, they were filled with stories of her students. I fear we may lose her to this backwoods hollow."

Asher's heart leaped. Dare he hope?

"Last I saw her, she was fine, ma'am."

The occupants of the wagon settled back into a silence broken only by the muted clomps of the horses' hooves. Asher loved Christmastime on the mountain. A new snow covering everything pristine and pure. What better way to start a new year than with the landscape also washed clean?

They passed his cabin, a lone candle burning in the window, Leroy's sign that all was well inside. Asher clicked to the horses to pick up the pace. "You'll see the cabin around that yonder bend."

"Our daughter is used to a big two-story house with servants. How she could ever say she was happy in a one-room cabin is beyond me, but Charlotte has always had a mind of her own." Mrs. Nelson laughed. "A trial and a joy, that girl. Oh, how I've missed her. Did she find a use for the things I sent?"

"Yes, ma'am. She turned them into costumes for the Christmas play. Her way of getting around the mountain people's views on charity. This way, the children keep the costumes and their parents can't be anything but grateful."

"Tell me, young man—" Mr. Nelson laid a hand on Asher's shoulder "—how has she really been? My girl has a way of finding trouble."

How much should Asher tell him? He didn't want to lie, but then again, he didn't want to betray Charlotte's trust. "The schoolhouse burned down. Charlotte's hands were mildly burned and scraped, but they're as good as new now."

Mrs. Nelson gasped. "How horrible."

"She's also proven to be a fine nurse. I caught pneumonia once, after searching for her when she got lost—"

"Lost? Oh, dear. Henry?"

"She's fine, dear. Charlotte's a strong woman, not a child." He patted his wife's hand. "So my daughter nursed you back to health?"

"Yes, sir. I might've died without her. She's also taken two orphaned children under her wings. You should be very proud of your daughter." Asher pulled in front of the cabin. "We're here."

"Just a moment." Mr. Nelson climbed from the wagon, helped his wife down, then turned back to Asher. "Would my daughter happen to be the woman you've set your eye on?"

Asher rubbed his chin. "Would that cause a problem, sir?"

"How does she feel about you?"

"I haven't asked. I plan to after the pageant tomorrow."

Her father exhaled sharply, his gaze not wavering from Asher's. "You seem like a good man, and I trust my daughter's judgment. Most of the time." His lips twitched. "If she wants you, then I give my blessing. I won't say a word until she says something to me." He thrust out his hand and shook Asher's. "Thank you for the ride."

Taking his wife's arm, Mr. Nelson led her to the front door and rapped three times. Asher watched as a lantern flickered to life inside. He should leave, but couldn't. He wouldn't be able to see Charlotte's face even with the moonlight, but he would be able to hear the pleasure in her voice.

The door opened, the light within highlighting Charlotte's form. "Mother? Papa?"

"Daughter, you can see right through your gown. It's indecent."

"This time of night, I thought a knock on the door

might be an emergency. I wasn't worried about my apparel."

"As everyone can tell." Mrs. Nelson guided Charlotte back inside and closed the door.

Asher laughed, the sound ringing through the night air.

Chapter 14

"I don't know why I have to wear this purple shirt." Matthew held it up, a look of disdain on his freckled face. "It's girlish."

"It is not. It's the color of royalty," Charlotte said, cupping his cheek. "You are a king."

"Top king?"

"I want to be top king," Mark asserted.

Charlotte shook her head. Obviously, the hastily erected curtain separating the cast members from the congregation didn't hold out very much sound. Laughter filled the church. "Shhh. You both have a very important part in today's play. The wise men were very significant in the Christmas story."

The baby Jesus chose that moment to wail. The youngest Jones child, still suffering from colic, was not happy with her swaddling clothes and fought to free herself, one chubby fist pumping the air.

Charlotte lifted her from the manger and paced the floor, guiding each of the children into their prospective positions. "First, we need the shepherds and the angels. Pastor Sweeney has clear notes on where to stop narrating so you can speak your lines or sing. After the play, those of you who had time to rewrite your readings will do so. We will close the program with the sheriff's carol. Any questions?"

Every hand went up. "Yes, Georgie?"

"Is there going to be dessert afterwards? My stomach is growling."

"I told you to finish your supper." Charlotte patted the baby's back a little harder.

"But I was too excited to eat then."

"Yes, there will be desserts." She could smell the baked goods from there. If the children got through the program with the sight of the desserts against the side wall, it would be a wonder.

"Frank, take your arm off Lucy's shoulders," Charlotte whispered. "We don't need any dramatics other than on stage if her father should see."

The boy stepped back and glanced over his shoulder.

"Lucy, take this child to her mother to be nursed. Maybe she'll make it through the program if she falls asleep." Charlotte handed the baby to the girl and peeked around the curtain.

Standing room only. Her parents and Asher occupied one of the front pews. Her heart soared. Her surprise and pleasure at seeing them on her doorstep last night couldn't be measured in words. After her mother's reprimand about answering the door without a robe, they'd both burst into tears and spent half the night talking.

Charlotte had made pallets on the floor for Georgie, Molly and herself, giving her bed to her parents. She'd woken that morning to the aroma of frying bacon and flapjacks, surprised that her mother could cook on a simple stove. But then, she hadn't always lived in the lap of luxury.

One glance at her watch sent Charlotte scurrying into action. "Places," she instructed. "Two minutes."

Children squeaked and dashed away. Molly's foot became entangled in the curtain, bringing it crashing to the floor. More laughter rang out from the audience. If nothing else, the play should be entertaining. Asher, bless his heart, dashed to set the curtain to rights.

Pastor Sweeney stepped up to his podium and frowned. He rubbed his hand over the broken corner and glared at the group of children. They all pointed at Charlotte.

"I'm sorry," she mouthed. "Here's a swath of purple fabric to cover it for now. I'll replace it, I promise."

"You're a menace, Miss Nelson." He opened his Bible. "I thank the Lord I wised up and started courting the Widow Slater. She knows how to behave like a lady."

Charlotte's eyes widened, then she snorted and covered her mouth, trying desperately to keep her laughter inside. It wouldn't do at all to burst into full-blown laughter seconds before the play started. Instead, she ducked her head and hurried to her seat at the side of the stage. She thanked God the pastor's attention had transferred to someone else. A marriage between the two of them would never have worked.

"Oh, wait." She leaped up and hurried to take the pretend baby Jesus from her mother and lay the sleeping infant in the manger. "Now we're ready to begin."

As soon as two children pulled the curtains aside, the pastor began reading from the Gospel of Luke, his nasal voice carrying to every corner of the church. Charlotte tried to immerse herself in her notes, but instead a giggle escaped her. Her head shot up and her gaze met the shocked one of her mother. Her pa's mouth twitched. Asher looked everywhere but at the stage. Heavens.

The choir's angelic voices rang out as she gave the Good News to the shepherds. Georgie proudly carried his shepherd's hook and bowed before the angel. When it was time to head to Bethlehem, and one of the smaller shepherds forgot to follow, Georgie promptly "hooked" him and led him to the proper place.

With a hand on the smaller boy's head, Georgie forced him to his knees. "Bow. This is God you're looking at."

Charlotte lost all restraint. Giggles burst forth like bubbles in a hot spring.

The three wise men stomped down the center aisle of the church, pretending to ride camels, their heads bobbing up and down so quickly, Charlotte was almost afraid one of the boys' heads would fall off and reach the stage before them. They placed gaily wrapped packages at the feet of Jesus while Pastor Sweeney continued his narration.

"I'm hot." Luke shrugged off his cloak. "I'm the king from the desert. I don't need a robe. Baby Jesus can have it." He let the yards of green fabric fall to the floor.

Charlotte clapped a hand over her mouth, her teary, joy-filled gaze meeting Asher's. Well, at least the Word of God was being read, the story of Jesus's birth washing over the congregation despite the children's antics. She loved every misspoken word and out-of-bound step. Didn't Jesus himself say to suffer the little children?

With the play's completion, the children took turns reading their compositions. They read everything from one-line blessings to full-page stories on how much Christmas meant to them. The stories brought fresh tears to Charlotte's eyes.

Throughout her childhood, Christmas morning had always arrived with mounds of presents under a freshly cut tree. Most of these children were lucky if they received one gift. They truly understood the meaning of the holiday. She spotted her mother wiping a tear away with a fine, monogrammed hankie. Charlotte's gift sat right there next to the man she loved. The fact that her parents didn't want to spend even one Christmas away from her was the best gift she could receive.

She transferred her gaze to Asher. *Almost.*

Asher stood and approached the stage, tugging at his tie. Breathe. He could do this. Taking a deep breath, he opened his mouth and the words to "O Holy Night" poured forth.

Not a murmur came from the congregation or the children behind him. Asher closed his eyes and lived in the words of the song, letting his faith burst forth. When he finished, silence remained, every eye glued to him.

"Who knew our sheriff had a voice like an angel!" someone yelled.

Then the congregation stood and applauded while the children bowed. Hoots and hollers rose until he thought the rafters would shake.

"That was beautiful, Asher. I think you've missed your calling." Charlotte moved to center stage and folded her hands in front of her. "That concludes our Christmas program. We hope you were blessed with the hard work of your children and have a clearer understanding of the true meaning of Christmas."

"Wait a minute, Miss Nelson." Hank rushed to the front of the church. "We've a gift for you."

She glanced at Asher. He shrugged, having no idea what the man had cooked up. Whatever it was had Hank beaming like a shining star.

Pastor Sweeney joined Hank and thrust out his hand. "Miss Nelson, citizens of Plumville…"

Hank grasped his hand. "This feud is over!"

Charlotte burst into tears and turned to Asher. He wrapped his arms around her, letting her tears soak the front of his shirt. "You did this, Charlotte. You and no one else." He tilted her face to his. "You reignited a light in Plumville that had died a long time ago." He turned her to face the crowd. "Three cheers for Miss Nelson and her wonderful students."

The hoots started again. Mr. and Mrs. Nelson looked dumbfounded, yet joined in with the applause, clearly unsure of how to respond to such a rowdy people. If only they knew how precious their daughter was to this town. If they did, it wouldn't occur to them to take her back to Savannah.

Asher stayed by Charlotte's side as the townspeople filed past, shaking her hand. When Hank and Duke approached her, she sobbed and hugged them, causing both of their faces to turn a bright red. Duke cleared his throat and hurried to Leah Slater's side.

"I'm so happy, I could die right now, and never want another thing," Charlotte exclaimed.

"Nothing?" Asher took her hands in his.

"That was a joy to behold." Mrs. Nelson gathered Charlotte in a hug. "Clearly, you have made a difference in these children's lives. The play was a bit unorthodox, but very enjoyable."

"The children remained true to who they are," Charlotte said. "I couldn't ask for more. When I first arrived here, I tried to change the people to fit what I thought they should be. Then, when I almost died twice, and they rallied to my aid, I discovered they're exactly how God created them to be. Proud and wonderful."

"Almost died?" Mrs. Nelson cut a glance at Asher. "We hadn't heard of that."

Asher gave a sheepish grin and stepped back, feeling like an outsider. He glanced over the Nelsons' heads, locating Leroy and the boys around the dessert table. There'd be a better time to tell Charlotte of his feelings. A time when they weren't surrounded by people. Spring was still months away.

"Brother." Leroy clapped him on the back. "That was the best singing I've heard you do. You been practicing?"

Asher shook his head. "That was all God. All I did was open my mouth." He took a slice of cake.

"The way that gal's parents are hovering around her," Leroy said, nodding toward Charlotte, "I'm guessing you've got sugarplum dreams in your head if you think she's going to stay past spring."

"Maybe so, but I'm still going to try to convince her." Asher bit into the lemon cake, the icing tart on his tongue. "More than one blessing, other than my singing, can happen this Christmas season."

"Sheriff." Pastor Sweeney, Leah on his arm, approached. "You did a fine job on that stage. I'd like to keep it going, if you don't mind. Leah suggested we start a choir for Sunday services, and the platform would be the most wonderful place for them to stand. I'd also like to ask you to be our choir director."

Leroy laughed. "Yep, we were just saying how it's

the season for blessings. Today's the perfect day to ask him, Pastor."

Asher's face heated, and the once-moist cake dried and stuck in his throat. Leroy thrust a mug of apple cider into his hand. Asher gulped the drink. "I'm not sure I can do a repeat performance."

"A gift like that shouldn't be wasted." Sweeney nodded. "You pray on it. Let me know. I'm sure your answer will be a positive one." He smiled down at Leah and headed toward another person to torment with his requests.

Asher grinned at his nephews. "Y'all want to help me play Santa? I've some crates from the Nelsons in my wagon. Two that go to Miss Nelson's, but the others are for the students."

"Yes, sir." The three dashed for the door, arguing over who would get the biggest and best.

Some things never changed. Asher met Charlotte's beaming gaze and waved. He'd see her tomorrow afternoon with a gift of his own. He patted his front breast pocket. One he hoped she'd receive with pleasure, simple though it might be.

"You're grinning like a fox." Leroy cocked his head. "More dreams?"

"Yes, brother." Asher nodded. "Very big ones."

Charlotte awoke on Christmas morning and stared into the fire. Flames of yellow and blue licked at the wood.

If the stirrings coming from the children's pallets meant anything, her morning calm wouldn't last long. She glanced at the packages under the tree, grateful for her parents' thoughtfulness. Not only had they brought her gifts, but toys and clothing for the children in her care and those who were her students. The parents couldn't refuse a Christmas gift, and every child left the church last night with something fun and useful.

And Charlotte had thought just a month ago, she'd be spending this special day alone. She smiled at the sight of the children's stockings hanging on the mantel. She'd purchased chalk, ribbons and a whistle, but could tell from the bulges that her mother had added to them.

She tossed aside her blankets and grabbed her robe. Maybe she could manage a cup of coffee before the day's festivities began.

"It's Christmas!" Molly raced to the tree. "We have presents. We've never had presents before. Look, our stockings are full."

Charlotte choked back a sob. Never had presents? She wrapped the little girl in a hug. She couldn't leave these children. Not ever. Nor could she leave Plumville. No, if Asher wouldn't have her, she'd remain a spinster and a mother to these two beautiful children. She'd earn enough for their keep by teaching. She glanced up to see tears in her mother's eyes. "I can't leave with you come summer."

"I know you can't." Mother sat in the rocker. "And I won't ask you to. You're needed here. Oh, but I do miss you when you're gone."

Georgie soon joined his sister, and Papa climbed from bed, heading immediately to get coffee started. "You two get into those socks hanging there. Presents can wait until I've woke up."

"Yes, sir." Georgie handed Molly hers and sat in front of the hearth to peer into his sock. "There's a whistle and a ball. A peppermint stick!"

Charlotte wiped her streaming eyes on her sleeve. How were the Thomas boys faring? She'd written of them so often, her parents had even brought an extra gift for each of them. She was truly blessed to have such loving parents. How could she have thought her mother sharp-tongued and unreasonable?

"It isn't proper to be sitting around in our night-clothes," her mother said. "Charlotte, we should dress for the day in case of company. Wear something festive."

"Yes, Mother." Charlotte stepped behind a quilt she'd hung for privacy and donned her new dress. *Please, Lord, say Asher will see me wearing the garment.* She didn't count overly much on him stopping by that day, especially with his brother's return. His family had their own day to celebrate. But a girl could hope.

When she'd finished dressing, she stepped out so her mother could dress. The contents of the children's socks were dumped on the floor, and unopened presents were already doled out to their prospective recipients, making traversing across the small cabin dangerous. Still, Charlotte grabbed a mug of coffee and made her way to a chair she could watch their faces as they unwrapped their gifts.

A knock sounded at the door. Her heart leaped. When it sounded again, she rushed to answer it.

"Hold it right there." Her mother stopped her. "A lady does not dash for the door. I'll answer it for you."

"Mother, please, this isn't Savannah."

A stern look had Charlotte sitting back in her seat and her mother allowing Asher entrance. "Merry Christmas." His gaze settled on her. "Uh, I've…hmmm." He glanced around the room.

"Perhaps you'd like to step outside?" Papa suggested, a twinkle in his eye.

"Charlotte, take your cloak," Mother said.

She didn't think she'd need one, not with the way Asher was looking at her, but rather than argue, Charlotte grabbed her wool cloak from a hook and brushed past Asher and outside.

"Merry Christmas, Asher. Thank you for dropping off the packages last night. You've made Georgie and Molly very happy. They've never—"

He pulled her to him, claiming her lips with his and shutting off her words. The world spun, swirling like the snowflakes falling around them. If not for Asher's arms holding her up, Charlotte would've fallen. He stepped back and put a finger to her lips. "No talking. I have something I need to say."

She nodded, her lips tingling.

"I love you, Charlotte Nelson." He knelt on the frozen ground. "I don't want you to go back to Savannah." He dug a simple gold band out of his pocket. "This was my mother's, and I want you to have it. Please, say you'll marry me. Your father has already—"

Charlotte threw her arms around him, knocking him backward until they both lay on the ground, the snow falling around them like kisses from heaven. This time, she kissed him until they were both breathless.

"It's about time you asked me, Asher Thomas." She grinned. "I was about to ask you instead."

"Charlotte Nelson! Get off the ground this instant." Mother stood, arms crossed, in the doorway.

"I guess she's been watching us," Asher whispered, his breath tickling Charlotte's ear. "Does this mean your answer is yes? If not, your mother will be completely scandalized at your inappropriate behavior."

Charlotte gave him a playful punch in the shoulder. "Of course it's a yes. How could you think otherwise?"

Asher pulled her to her feet, and Charlotte held out

her hand. "Wear this on your right hand until we marry. I'm not sure I can wait until your contract is up in the spring."

"Go back in the house, Mother." Charlotte blinked away tears as she gazed into Asher's hazel eyes. "I'm about to do something scandalous."

"Mercy." Mother slammed the door.

Charlotte cupped Asher's face in her hands. "The moment a replacement teacher arrives, I'll marry you. I'll inform the school board as soon as I can mail a letter. Right now, I'm going to kiss you breathless."

"Forward woman." He pulled her closer, and lowered his head.

Charlotte wasn't sure, but if asked, she'd say she heard violins playing.

* * * * *

REQUEST YOUR FREE BOOKS!

2 FREE CHRISTIAN NOVELS
PLUS 2
FREE
MYSTERY GIFTS

HEARTSONG
PRESENTS

HSPDIR13R

REQUEST YOUR FREE BOOKS!

2 FREE INSPIRATIONAL NOVELS
PLUS 2
FREE
MYSTERY GIFTS

Love Inspired
HISTORICAL
INSPIRATIONAL HISTORICAL ROMANCE

YES! Please send me 2 FREE Love Inspired® Historical novels and my 2 FREE mystery gifts (gifts are worth about $10). After receiving them, if I don't wish to receive any more books, I can return the shipping statement marked "cancel." If I don't cancel, I will receive 4 brand-new novels every month and be billed just $4.74 per book in the U.S. or $5.24 per book in Canada. That's a savings of at least 21% off the cover price. It's quite a bargain! Shipping and handling is just 50¢ per book in the U.S. and 75¢ per book in Canada.* I understand that accepting the 2 free books and gifts places me under no obligation to buy anything. I can always return a shipment and cancel at any time. Even if I never buy another book, the two free books and gifts are mine to keep forever.

102/302 IDN F5CY

Name	(PLEASE PRINT)	
Address		Apt. #
City	State/Prov.	Zip/Postal Code

Signature (if under 18, a parent or guardian must sign)

Mail to the **Harlequin® Reader Service:**
IN U.S.A.: P.O. Box 1867, Buffalo, NY 14240-1867
IN CANADA: P.O. Box 609, Fort Erie, Ontario L2A 5X3

Want to try two free books from another series?
Call 1-800-873-8635 or visit www.ReaderService.com.

* Terms and prices subject to change without notice. Prices do not include applicable taxes. Sales tax applicable in N.Y. Canadian residents will be charged applicable taxes. Offer not valid in Quebec. This offer is limited to one order per household. Not valid for current subscribers to Love Inspired Historical books. All orders subject to credit approval. Credit or debit balances in a customer's account(s) may be offset by any other outstanding balance owed by or to the customer. Please allow 4 to 6 weeks for delivery. Offer available while quantities last.

Your Privacy—The Harlequin® Reader Service is committed to protecting your privacy. Our Privacy Policy is available online at www.ReaderService.com or upon request from the Harlequin Reader Service.

We make a portion of our mailing list available to reputable third parties that offer products we believe may interest you. If you prefer that we not exchange your name with third parties, or if you wish to clarify or modify your communication preferences, please visit us at www.ReaderService.com/consumerschoice or write to us at Harlequin Reader Service Preference Service, P.O. Box 9062, Buffalo, NY 14269. Include your complete name and address.

REQUEST YOUR FREE BOOKS!

2 FREE INSPIRATIONAL NOVELS
PLUS 2
FREE
MYSTERY GIFTS

Love Inspired

YES! Please send me 2 FREE Love Inspired® novels and my 2 FREE mystery gifts (gifts are worth about $10). After receiving them, if I don't wish to receive any more books, I can return the shipping statement marked "cancel." If I don't cancel, I will receive 6 brand-new novels every month and be billed just $4.74 per book in the U.S. or $5.24 per book in Canada. That's a savings of at least 21% off the cover price. It's quite a bargain! Shipping and handling is just 50¢ per book in the U.S. and 75¢ per book in Canada.* I understand that accepting the 2 free books and gifts places me under no obligation to buy anything. I can always return a shipment and cancel at any time. Even if I never buy another book, the two free books and gifts are mine to keep forever.

105/305 IDN F49N

Name	(PLEASE PRINT)	
Address		Apt. #
City	State/Prov.	Zip/Postal Code

Signature (if under 18, a parent or guardian must sign)

Mail to the **Harlequin® Reader Service:**
IN U.S.A.: P.O. Box 1867, Buffalo, NY 14240-1867
IN CANADA: P.O. Box 609, Fort Erie, Ontario L2A 5X3

**Are you a subscriber to Love Inspired books
and want to receive the larger-print edition?
Call 1-800-873-8635 or visit www.ReaderService.com.**

* Terms and prices subject to change without notice. Prices do not include applicable taxes. Sales tax applicable in N.Y. Canadian residents will be charged applicable taxes. Offer not valid in Quebec. This offer is limited to one order per household. Not valid for current subscribers to Love Inspired books. All orders subject to credit approval. Credit or debit balances in a customer's account(s) may be offset by any other outstanding balance owed by or to the customer. Please allow 4 to 6 weeks for delivery. Offer available while quantities last.

Your Privacy—The Harlequin® Reader Service is committed to protecting your privacy. Our Privacy Policy is available online at www.ReaderService.com or upon request from the Harlequin Reader Service.
We make a portion of our mailing list available to reputable third parties that offer products we believe may interest you. If you prefer that we not exchange your name with third parties, or if you wish to clarify or modify your communication preferences, please visit us at www.ReaderService.com/consumerschoice or write to us at Harlequin Reader Service Preference Service, P.O. Box 9062, Buffalo, NY 14269. Include your complete name and address.

LIDIR13R